Mother Country

ELISABETH RUSSELL TAYLOR

Mother Country

PETER OWEN · LONDON

PETER OWEN PUBLISHERS
73 Kenway Road London SW5 0RE

First published in Great Britain 1992
© Elisabeth Russell Taylor

A catalogue record for this book is available
from the British Library

ISBN 0–7206–0848–1

Printed in Great Britain by Billings of Worcester

Contents

Mother   7

Charlotte   57

Walter   89

Resolution   131

Post-Mortem   149

Postscript   167

I am indebted to the Authors' Foundation for the generous grant given me for the writing of this book.

E.R.T.

Mother

I have never come across anyone in whom the moral
sense was dominant who was not heartless, cruel,
vindictive, log-stupid and entirely lacking in the smallest
sense of humanity. Moral people, as they are termed,
are simple beasts.

Oscar Wilde

IT IS EMBALMED IN MY THOUGHTS. IT IS AS IF MY ENTIRE EARLY
life were distilled in that one summer's afternoon and evening. It
was a particularly hot afternoon and I had arrived at the cross-roads
feeling oppressed by the heat, but as soon as I turned into the
avenue, I felt cold; there was always damp air trapped beneath the
nave of plane trees that extended from one end of the road to
the other. The perfect Gothic arch precluded sunlight and lent
the asphalt a dull pewter aspect, making me think of images of the
Styx.

I was early. I had agreed to present myself at three-thirty for tea
and it was only five minutes past the hour. I had twenty-five
minutes to fill and so I wandered very slowly along the avenue,
stopping to peer over the gates at each of the large Edwardian
houses set back in their immaculately groomed grounds. I was
struck by the note of imperialism that resonated from the architecture, and by the manner in which the garden planting confirmed that authority by extending it to the strict control of nature.

Despite the disagreeable circumstances that had combined to
force me back to the avenue after more than twenty years –
twenty years during the course of which I had avoided coming
within five miles even of the neighbourhood – I was neither
particularly displeased nor apprehensive: I was indifferent. Indeed,
it was because I found myself indifferent that I had yielded effort-
lessly to my sister's pleas: 'I think you really ought . . . she's very

little time left . . . she may have things she wants to say to you . . .
you may have things. . . .'

What the hell, I had thought, replacing the receiver and noting
the arrangement in my diary.

I was so conscious of the sound of my shoes crunching the
gravel in the silence of the drive that I quickly turned on to one of
the several brick paths which cut across the front garden and led
eventually to the pillared porch with its double doors. In my
childhood the garden had been my refuge. I had loved it in all its
aspects, and in every season: the secret places under the flowering currants where, even in the suffocating heat of summer, the
ground was soggy and the scents of the earth unfathomably delicious; the sun-drenched beds of sweet peas, cistus and pinks, on
whose combined heady scents I became intoxicated. In autumn, I
had been especially drawn to the gnarled apple trees in the orchard
behind the house; one or two stubborn fruits always lingered to
ripen on inaccessible branches, and beneath the trees windfalls
rotted into the ground, helped on by armies of hard-working
insects. In spring, narcissus and daffodils that had naturalized under
the trees spattered the lush grass with a creamy foam. Always, the
garden gave me a taste of freedom.

However, even in the garden there were things to puzzle me.
Why had Father placed stone figures with full jugs, cornucopias
and breasts eternally on the verge of spilling their bounty over our
land? What did those who extended a beckoning finger want from
me? And did the fish in the pond know that the windows through
which they darted were merely a reflection of those in the
summer-house by the water's edge?

Jane Austen wrote that one does not love a place the less for
having suffered in it. My refuge had earned the right to call itself
my Eden long years before I was expelled from it.

Today procumbent plants strayed before my feet as I made my
way towards the front door. The dazzling abundance of carefully
matched and mixed colours and forms made me wonder whether
Mr Henderson, the gardener, and his two assistants were still alive
and in my mother's employ. Inescapably, I found myself wandering
along the length of the lavender path that led on to the summer-
house. As I inhaled the scent and watched the bees in their
obsessive quest for nectar, a wave of memory poised to break over
me. I struggled to restrain it. I knew that I must find the strength to

raise a sea-wall against all recollection: not a single memory must seep through the barricade, for it was only my capacity for repressing the past that ensured my present indifference. Yet, automatically, I came to a standstill in front of the bush of *Liebchen* roses – flowers that 'had the look of flowers that are looked at'.

It was three thirty-five. Charlotte would notice and appreciate the five minutes' grace I had allowed for manners, the five minutes that would permit my disingenuous sister, if she chose, to 'forget the time', or be surprised to find that my expected arrival had 'slipped her memory'.

The front-door bell clanged loud, so loud that I wondered if perhaps the household was manned by the hard of hearing.

'Miss Charlotte is expecting you.' The parlourmaid's voice was expressionless. How long had she been in the service of my family? Did she know? Was she privy to the shameful secret that, ordinarily, I did not visit? 'Miss Charlotte is in the library.'

And as she crossed the parquet to open the library door, Charlotte emerged from it. Wordlessly, with trumped-up concern and devotion, she placed her hands on my upper arms and leant to kiss me on both cheeks.

'My dear. It's been a long, long time. . . . Much too long.'

The final 'much too long' was added with full dramatic force, after a pause pregnant with a sorrow I knew she did not feel. Then, pushing me away from her, holding me at arms' length, she appraised me. I could detect in her gaze an old, familiar disapproval; her tender camouflaging accents of concern made me all the more conscious of it. I had not met with such insincerity since last I was in this house and under her inspection.

'*Tant mieux!*' she sighed reluctantly. 'You've arrived in time.'

I had not wished to be kissed. I had not wished to be touched. I could have done without any display of emotion. I was conscious of my abiding sense of estrangement.

'Tea in the drawing-room, Madge.' For this instruction Charlotte adopted a different tone of voice: that of the chatelaine. I imagined she had taken over the running of the house and garden even before Mother fell ill. Was her commanding tone one that families like mine order from the catalogue from which they select their servants' uniforms?

Charlotte glided ahead of me and pushed open the drawing-room door. The blinds were lowered to half-mast. I was immediately transported to a previous existence. Although the drawing-room faced south, it was a sombre room, made more funereal in summer when the blinds were lowered to prevent direct light fading the mahogany and the blue damask curtains. The lid of the Bechstein was open, the piano-stool pushed back as if only recently vacated, and the doors of the music cabinet were open. A luxuriant philodendron, apparently growing straight from the plinth on which it had been placed, was the only object in the room with a mind of its own. Everything else was manifestly subject to the Sinclair mood and will.

The house had always been fastidiously maintained. If any one of the servants proved anything but relentless in her pursuit of dust and dirt, she was sacked. But no matter the efforts of the army of cleaners to sterilize the atmosphere, the drawing-room, dining-room and library always looked dingy. The walls – painted ochre, or darkly panelled – were hung with tapestries and uninspired Victorian paintings. The divans in the drawing-room were strewn with Persian rugs and an assortment of worn *gros point* cushions, the colours of which suggested that dust had been beaten into rather than out of them. When the dining-room table was not laid, it was garnished with a faded velvet and brocade runner made even more colourless by the shining brightness of the two silver candelabra that held it in position. The plush on the chairs and the plush draping the windows both gave the impression of age and wear: of the past, and of another country, Mother's.

Only the library had been different. Father's retreat. Here the verdigris of tradition coloured everything. It was the only emphatically English room in the house. It had about it something of a gentleman's club in some far-flung colony: leather-topped desk, worn and spattered with ink; wicker chairs; golf-clubs, a tennis-racket with strings broken, a polo-stick, horsewhip and riding boots in the corner. A plate of curled Marmite sandwiches and a bottle of Highland Malt on a bamboo table; photographs of minor royalty presenting a cup.

Nothing about the house had ever suggested the existence of children. Our bicycles and scooters, our dolls' prams and wheelbarrows, the wigwam (the one possession I truly loved) – these toys were kept in a shed at the back of the orchard and were all tidied away out of sight as soon as we had been hurried off to bed. When the weather was unsuitable for play in the open, we were confined to the nursery on the top floor of the house, along the passage that led to the maids' rooms in one direction and our little bedrooms in the other. The toys we played with inside the house were not permitted in the garden, and vice versa.

I walked across the drawing-room on Charlotte's heels. She raised one of the blinds and we stood side by side, looking out of the window. There before us on the porch was the garden furniture. But something was wrong. It was not the old green swinging hammock and park bench and iron chairs. . . . It was garish; heavy wood painted chalk-white, with plastic cushions patterned with multicoloured flowers of a species unknown in nature.

'A Christmas present from Uncle Harold, I'm afraid. And naturally we shan't be able to dispose of them so long as he's alive.' I laughed to myself, for I knew that this must create an insuperable dilemma for Charlotte: appearances and family loyalty (as they called it) both high on her list of priorities and here in conflict. Charlotte could not cope with anything vulgar; a vulgar object was to her a continuous babble of obscenity, she had once told me.

'How is Uncle Harold?' I inquired.

'Much the same. Do you take sugar?'

'And lemon.'

'He warned Mother just before Christmas that something very special – "the best that money can buy" – was on its way from Harrods. Mother has closed her Harrods account. She refers to the store as "the souk" and wasn't the least surprised by the unsuitability of her brother's paraphernalia. We kept it concealed under a tarpaulin until June.'

While Charlotte drank tea ruminatively I thought of Uncle Harold, for the first time for many years. Mother's bachelor brother was much like a Tudor queen: he paraded his wealth for all to see.

I had brought Charlotte a present of some camellia oil for the *lampe bergère*. Although she accepted my offering with formal gratitude, I could see that it did not go down very well and she would undoubtedly pass it on to a charity next Christmas. I sat facing her, hypnotized by her facial expressions and trying to decipher her penetrating stares and darting glances. She had grown rather fat and was wearing a shapeless garment of flowered silk, no doubt to conceal her surplus flesh. She had fine features, but she so lacked style that I was sure they passed unremarked. She had settled into a caricature of the spinster daughter, left to care devotedly for the aged parent. As she spoke, I was struck by the way she managed to appear inquisitive without being genuinely curious, and busy without being vital. This was nothing new, though; she had always been an automaton, wound up by Father and Mother.

'It won't be long now. She's become very weak these past few days. Her mind's gone. It's not that she's senile – far from it. It's just that she's confused, lost all sense of time. Yesterday and fifty years ago are all the same. Yesterday she spoke as if she were back in Baden-Baden. It was 1920 for her. Promise me, Antonia, you'll allow her her fantasies?'

I answered by not taking issue and drinking my tea.

Loyal, lying-to-the-last Charlotte! She had never learnt that to do the right thing for the wrong reason is morally more reprehensible than to do the wrong thing for the right reason. And this was not the moment to point it out.

'Cook will be so hurt if you don't try a piece of her walnut gâteau,' she whined.

And it came back to me. It was all very well for the cook to be overworked and underpaid, and allocated an unheated bedroom and, when she prepared lobster thermidor for the dining-room, to prepare 'nice cod steaks' for the kitchen, but it was unpardonable for one of the children to leave her cake untried.

I accepted two slices of walnut cake. It was excellent. While I gratefully ate, I was spared having to talk to Charlotte, who prattled on about staff (problems of obtaining them in the first place and retaining them in the second), her charity work for distressed musicians, and the exorbitant cost of day-and-night nursing care for Mother.

'I did what I could, Antonia. I did what I could until I was dropping,' she insisted, making believe that I would think the less of her for getting in professional help. 'But I find Mother too heavy to lift. And she has become terribly demanding. The sick and dying do, you know.'

I am not sure that I did know, but I was struck that Mother, who had always been notoriously demanding, had become too much so for Charlotte. I wondered what form her demands had taken.

'I shall leave you to find your own way,' Charlotte said, rising, indicating that the time had come for me to undertake the filial duty she had imposed upon me. She walked back to the window again to distract herself with the ghastliness of Uncle Harold's garden furniture. When I left the drawing-room, it was Charlotte's back that was turned towards me. We had met and spoken as strangers, for that was what we were and had always been – and would remain.

As I slowly mounted the stairs, I was struck by the unnecessarily thick pile on the Chinese blue Wilton, the too-wide and too-deep treads, the too-richly carved and too-keenly polished balustrade, and the over-abundance of pictures on the walls of the staircase. From the ground to the second floor, the walls were hung with family portraits, highly varnished likenesses of the fearsome military men and their plain, sensible women who were my paternal forebears.

My parents' house had always been bathed in silence rather than quiet. Neither of them could distinguish between peace and stagnation. The merest sound was absorbed by the carpets, the heavy and perfectly fitting mahogany doors and the panelled walls. The command 'Quiet, child!' – issued in a stage whisper – came back to me. Charlotte and I had both been expected to observe a deathly hush on our parents' premises. Nothing of that had changed. As I stepped on to the first-floor landing, I saw the handle on the door of the master bedroom turn. A nurse slipped from behind it with a tray of tablets, and I slipped in, closing the door soundlessly behind me.

In her sarcophagus, her marriage sarcophagus, the old woman, my mother, who was completing the journey from newness to negation, who carried into marriage and motherhood her childhood and adolescence with no thought of modulating into maturity, was swaddled for death. All that was left of her physically were her orange-peel skin, her wire-wool hair and her beady eyes. And round about her, still, were that cleanliness and order which had throughout her existence occupied the place that passion might have filled.

'Mother.' I called her name quietly, partly from habit, and partly because I should have preferred not to be heard, and not to receive a response. 'Mother,' I felt obliged to repeat. 'It's me, Antonia.' I placed the *Liebchen* rose in a tumbler of water on her bedside table. I noticed that a bony claw had emerged from the bedclothes and was clutching the coverlet.

'Antonia?' She sounded surprised, even incredulous. Surely Charlotte must have told her I was expected? 'Let me see you, my child.'

Child. My child. How dare she! No more 'child' than she 'Mother' . . . never a child, not really. Never the occasion: no childhood; no mothering. Just because she bore me gives her no right to call me her child and consider herself my mother: it's nurture that accords that right. It's not enough for her to have opened her legs and dispelled me from her womb into the world. She should have opened her heart and held me fast.

Melancholy overcame me. A veil descended, obscuring the outside world. All was lost without its ever having been found. Now she would never listen to me, laugh with me, offer me a present. She would never confide in me, teach me, provide me with a safe haven. . . .

'I'm dying.'

'I know.'

'I've something to say to you.'

I wished she hadn't.

'I have an apology . . .'

Too late! Much too late.

'You see, I never cared for children.'

Too true. I dragged a chair from under the window overlooking the orchard. I put it beside the bed. I was consumed with fatigue, a sort of paralysing lassitude had overcome me.

Mother struggled to raise herself on her elbows. (All the better to see you with. . . .) 'Help me!' she demanded, adding: 'The nurses won't. They're Australian.'

I recognized at once the peculiar blend of snobbishness and irritability that characterized her.

'Put the pillow behind my back. Plump it.'

But I sat firm. I could find neither the strength nor the willingness to help her, for that would have involved physical contact. I had not touched her since I was tiny and I wasn't going to start again now. She was skeletal (of course, Charlotte could *easily* have raised her with one hand), and her flesh *feuillemorte*. If I were to help her to raise herself a little, she might well snap and crumble in my hands, adding terror to my distaste. Fortunately she forgot almost at once what she had asked me. She fell back, but not before she had caught sight of the rose.

'*Ach! Ach!* A *Liebchen* rose. Child. You remember Walter?'

She pronounced Walter *Valter*, and with her *Ach! Ach!*, to which I knew she would inevitably add a *so*, I remembered not only the man to whom she referred but how, after fifty years' living in England, many of them with an English husband, my mother remained resolutely Baden-Baden and proud of it.

'He adored me, you know. I was the only one in his life. We shared so much. Charlotte won't let me mention his name. I can't understand why. *Lächerlich!*

Oh dear. What a pity that Charlotte, who had taken every fence for forty-five years, had refused the final one.

'Of course Walter was never very interested in Charlotte, was he? He adored *me*. You know how he adored me, don't you, Antonia? Kept your father on his toes!' And Mother cackled. '*Liebchen* roses . . .'

Beloved Walter. . . . I shall never tell you, Mother, and you will never know. And far from keeping Father on his toes, he rendered him supine . . .

'*Liebchen* roses! You could call them our signature tune. I'll tell you a secret, Antonia . . .'

Please! No secrets. Above all, no secrets!

'When we were children, Walter and I, no more than eleven or twelve, playing in the park at Schloss Huberman, one day Walter pricked his finger and then pricked mine with a thorn he tore from a *Liebchen* rose. He mixed our blood. "Whatever befalls us," he said, "we shall always be one." And then he kissed me, passionately, for the first time, and from that day on we remained forever linked.'

The past lay perilously close, just behind my eyes. Adhering to it was remembrance kept at bay by a mere coat of translucent preservative. Blood ties. Roses.

I am twelve. All blood ties in my life have been severed. Since the age of nine, when war broke out, I have been at boarding-school four hundred miles from London. Most holidays I am confined here, too, or sent to holiday schools. The bombing is blamed for my exile. Charlotte is with distant and unknown relatives in America; they had accommodation for only one more child. Father is missing, presumed dead. Mother and Uncle Harold left London after the Battle of Britain and are evading the authorities, and hence all war work, and are in lodgings in Stroud. They have located a farm within walking distance where, for not inconsiderable sums of money, they are able to procure an abundance of butter, bacon and eggs. 'We hardly know there's a war on,' Mother boasts.

I have failed to make friends at school. I do not attend morning assembly, nor do I join the crocodile to church on Sundays. I have been informed by a pupil with orange hair and freckles named Valerie that, according to her father, the war is all the fault of the Jews. Out of filial respect, no doubt, Valerie has introduced my skull suddenly and intimately to the concrete on the playground. She stunned me, and I was confined to the sick-room for two weeks. I learn that there is no hiding from the likes of Valerie. Despite my impeccably English surname, Valerie detected something alien about me and, what is more, warned the rest of the school of their possible contamination. Only an educationally subnormal evacuee, a little younger than I (who is intellectually incapable of grasping the infamy of Jewishness), wants to be my friend. I reject her. Every child knows that an outcast cannot become the intimate of another outcast. Far from becoming acceptable, the two of us would arouse suspicion and attract further persecution. But there is nothing I can do to dissuade Susie from pursuing me.

It is Sunday morning. Because she is incapable of keeping quiet, Susie is forbidden church. (I did wonder about this at the time. I knew enough about Jesus to feel he would have overlooked Susie's chattering.) She shadows me as I cross the tennis-courts and run down the bank to the area allotted to pupils' garden plots. She watches closely while I cut all the blooms from my *Liebchen* rose-bush, a bush I have succeeded in growing from a cutting taken from home. She lollops along behind me, her poor uncoordinated limbs thrashing the air, back into the house, where she stands too close and too wildly by my side in the pantry, peering while I soak tissue-paper in the sink and enfold each rose stalk in a white shroud before placing it carefully next to another in a shoe-box.

'Putting them to bed?' she inquires and, when I fail to reply, confidently and excitedly shouts: 'Putting them in their coffin, then!'

Mother's letter starts with a description of the dreariness of provincial life in England. Life in Stroud is something she is neither used to nor equipped to deal with, nor does she wish to become used to it or equip herself for it. She ends: 'The roses arrived dead. Please do not send more. Remember, Antonia, it is I who pay the postage.'

'I should have waited for him. I know that, now. *Na ja*.' And here Mother adopted a sickeningly confiding tone. 'But I was so impetuous when I was young. I was a great beauty, Antonia. You should have seen me. All the young men were after me. Mother used to say: "Lisa, my darling, how *will* you choose?"'

While Mother dreamt of her youth and beauty and elaborated on both to me, I thought back to the photograph albums in the bureau. They told a rather different story. Mother as a child, a young woman and a young mother: not pretty at all! Large-boned, heavy, slightly masculine looking; coarse features, coarse hair and skin. But, it has to be said, always rescued from the careless indifference of nature by man's taste and skill – always dressed in well-cut clothes set off with exquisite antique jewellery.

I am eight.

'I wish . . . I always expected a *pretty* daughter. . . . At least your sister's clever. My advice to you, Antonia, is this: see to it that you are always clean, tidy and punctual.' Mother is combing my hair. She is pulling at the knots. She is hurting me. 'When I was your age, complete strangers used to stop *my* mother in the street and compliment her on my appearance.'

Like thistles, her words scratch me; like needles, they penetrate.

I was fully grown up, doing my first degree at London University, when one day I found myself wandering through the oriental silks at Liberty's. I was roused from my reverie when I became conscious of an exchange taking place between a mother and daughter.

'You look lovely in both, darling. You shall have both! Let's go to the ground floor straight away and pick out some corals to match.'

'Oh Mummy, what a lovely idea! Thank you so much. Corals would go perfectly.'

I panicked; I feared I was going to scream. My tear-filled eyes obscured my vision and I walked into a cheval looking-glass that held the reflection of the beautiful daughter and the loving mother. I cut my cheek just below the eye. Somewhere, I thought, there's another life. . . .

'Rubinstein told Papa that I had the makings of a *great* pianist. But Papa didn't want that for me. He was tone-deaf, you see. He didn't like the piano being played constantly in the house. He told me: "Lisa, my plan for you is a good marriage with a man of rank and reputation. *Wie man sich bettet so liegt man.*"'

Walter Huberman, the man whom Mother did not marry, the man whose rank and reputation had not impressed my grandfather Bergner, proved as influential in her life and mine as the man she did marry, my father, whose rank and reputation had, on the contrary, so greatly impressed Grandfather.

I hoped that Mother was not going to discuss Walter with me. I knew more than I needed to know already, and I had learnt it from Walter himself.

Walter Huberman had been the youngest of the five sons of a Frankfurt banker. Four sons followed their father and their grandfather into the bank but Walter made it clear from earliest childhood that he had other plans. From childhood he developed a mind of his own and the firm determination to lead a life of pleasure. He was quickly dubbed a ne'er-do-well, a bounder with charm. This was not an accusation that would ever have been levelled against my father. Walter had looks, Father had not. Walter also had debts where Father had none – and never would have. Walter was in debt from the age of five, when he borrowed from the groom. He explained how this transaction would work to the benefit of the groom; he explained 'interest' to the man, having absorbed the jargon of banking almost from the time he was weaned, if not the subtler requisites for the job. Later in life he would become indebted to his tailor, his vintner and his landlord. However, the term 'bounder' is mutable, dependent upon contemporary values and customs. Whereas Walter seemed to fit the description in my grandfather's generation, he appeared 'continental' to my father's, and to mine romantic and heroic. Walter knew how to enjoy himself, and I had enough experience of the English to know the truth of the French observation that *le fond du caractère anglais, c'est l'absence de bonheur* and to want to distance myself from it. Walter knew how to turn every day into a festival. He knew how to listen, how to make his companion of the moment think well of himself. At the time, I did not suspect him of self-interest but regarded him as a midshipman lashed to the mast in a raging storm, intent upon locating land and summoning rescue for his friend.

'Call the nurse!' I had no need to ask Mother why she suddenly required the nurse. My parents had always recoiled from anything that related to the human orifices. In their revulsion, they held that the mouth should never be opened wide, neither for the intake of food nor for the expulsion of reproach. Regarding the function of the anus, it was tantamount to non-existent – judging from the manner in which they slipped in and out of the lavatory, as if conducting an immoral and illicit relationship. And the vagina. . . . Given the complexities surrounding its function, its accessibility to immoral as much as moral use, and thus its inherent frailty, it was better ignored altogether.

When the nurse tiptoed back into the bedroom, I tiptoed out. I stood on the landing, overlooking the banisters.

When I was a child, the landings held the same strategic advantage for me as a hill commanding a battle front for a look-out. Crouching here, I could see into the hall without being seen; I could hear without being heard. I saw and heard all the skirmishes. And there were many. As I stood mournfully there now like one shut out, waiting for the nurse to administer the bedpan and leave Mother's room, I recalled how often in my childhood I had peered down, terrified, into the hall. Mother was always weeping. Father would be scarlet in the face, raging quietly. Walter's name bounced off the furniture. And then my gaze would come to rest on the door leading to the kitchen quarters.

I am happiest in the kitchen with Cook. I am always welcome here, even though I am so small. However much I stretch up, I cannot reach the bowl to scrape out the cake mixture. Cook has to lift me on to the table. Cook is washing up at the sink. I am absorbed, alternately tracing patterns in the mixture and scooping out the remains with my finger into my mouth.

Suddenly Cook turns. 'Quick! Your mother's on the warpath!' She gathers me in her arms, wiping my mouth with her apron, and puts me down on the floor. I crawl under the table.

'Cook! I want to discuss the menu for. . . .' But before she has time to specify for which dinner party, she spots me. 'How many times have I told you *not* to bother Cook!' She fishes under the table, grabs my arm and drags me out and along the windowless corridor. 'I will not tolerate this disobedience.'

I have not managed to get to my feet, and my arm feels as if it is coming away from my shoulder.

Mother stops at the green baize door. 'Nanny! Nanny! Get the key to the broom cupboard from Mrs Rudge.'

I go cold. I know what is in store for me. 'Please, Mummy, please! Don't lock me up. Not in there!' I am shaking hysterically. The dark, dusty cupboard and its contents are all too familiar, yet it is a terrifying place. There is a mousetrap with a piece of cheese in one corner, and in another a tin of some gluey substance that sticks to my clothes. There is a bristly broom that scratches my legs and a mop-head that smells of sick.

'Perhaps that will teach you to do as your mother says! I will not stand for this insubordination! I wish. . . .'

Inside the cupboard I narrow my shoulders to make myself as small as possible, so that I do not brush up against unidentifiable things. I sit on an upturned bucket, my feet off the ground to avoid the cockroaches. When Father comes home, I shall be let out of the cupboard to be given a sound hiding.

'And Charlotte tells me you are a professor. Good gracious me! Of what, may I ask?'

'Archaeology. But I am not a professor. I am thirty-eight years of age, Mother. I've not done too badly becoming a senior lecturer.' Parental neglect has been a powerful spur . . .

'Archaeology,' Mother murmured. 'That's a funny thing for a woman to be doing – digging. And you've not married?'

'No.'

'What a pity! *Natürlich* women with professions often don't. Men don't like career women. It's not feminine . . .'

'Did you enjoy being married, Mother?'

'Really, Antonia, what a funny question! Of course I did. I had a position in life. I had this lovely home.' A gilded cage is none the less a cage. . . . 'Don't you miss this home?'

What a dirty word is home! Old people's, children's, mental . . . all places of cruelty and neglect. Homework, home-truths. . . . And to be at home, a lingering dissolution . . .

'No, I can't say I miss this home.' When I thought about it at all, I concluded that one did not have to go to prison to live in solitary confinement. What an impenetrable fortress of ignorance home was. A world in which everything that was not compulsory was forbidden and all judgements were spiteful; in which every idea that did not originate with Father and Mother was dismissed as being absurd or immoral.

'Charlotte loves her home. But you and she were always so different. People used to say it was as if you belonged to different families. From the day she was born, Charlotte somehow fitted in, and from the day you were born, you didn't. D'you know what? You even refused the breast.'

From her tone, I could hear that all these years later my mother still smarted at this proof of my insolence. If I had ever known that I had refused the breast, I had forgotten it. But what an appropriate act of defiance! The tiny creature that was me, emerging from the unknown so knowing. My transgression, my taste for independence, as old as myself, accompanying me as indelibly as a strawberry mark. Had I, I wondered, disliked her womb as much as I subsequently disliked her body? Had she infected me before I was formed? Had she gestated me emotionally handicapped, and had I recoiled within her as I recoiled without? For I recalled with clarity how young I had been when first I registered my repugnance for her body.

She is stepping out of the bath on to a black-and-white chequered mat. I am seated on the laundry-bin. The bin has a soft inlaid lid made from cork, and I enjoy the warm feel of it on the back of my thighs. Mother is standing a little apart from me, her arms outstretched, pulling her bath towel across her back. I note that her neck is red with weals, her stomach crazy-paved with scars. Between her legs there is hair, mangy stuff, not like the coarse hair on her head, more like the hair in her armpits and the stuff that oozes out of the old sofa in the maids' sitting-room. Why does she have hair there? I don't. Her breasts hang like half-filled cream-cheese bags – like the ones Cook hangs over the sink in the pantry. Do they make cheese, too? Suddenly I feel sick. I get up on to the laundry-bin lid, lean over the basin and I am sick. The smell of sick mingles with the smell of Mother's French Fern soap.

'Run the tap, child!' Mother bellows. 'Run the tap!' Her voice is furious. 'Filthy little animal!' Perhaps I do not hear all she has to say, for I run out of the bathroom as quickly as I can and slam the door behind me.

The noise of that door slamming rings now in my ears, so eloquent it was, given the embargo on noise.

'Charlotte's always such a comfort. Tell her to bring me a tisane. And do tell her to bring it up herself. I don't want Madge in here.'

'Mother wants a tisane.' Charlotte rose and moved across the drawing-room to the bell-pull by the chimney-piece. She returned to the table at which she had been seated and to the photograph album that lay open there.

'Do you remember the day that was taken?'

I looked down. I remembered all right. I felt emptied and slightly dizzy. Mother is dressed in the then-fashionable wide slacks and striped jumper; Father is wearing Oxford bags; Charlotte and I are in bathing costumes. Charlotte is standing between our parents, clutching bucket, spade, beach-ball and ice-cream. I am crouched in front of the group. I have a little stick of some sort in my hand, and am tracing patterns in the sand that has been wind-swept on to the promenade.

'Yes, I remember that day well.' And since that day I have often thought how dearly I should like to own a single photograph of my mother with her arm around me.

The place is Cromer. We are staying at The Grand for two weeks in August. We have a suite of rooms: two bedrooms, a sitting-room and a bathroom. Father hires a beach-hut. He likes to sit protected from the elements, looking out over the North Sea through his binoculars, and Mother likes to read sentimental novels, of which Father is disdainful, and write letters to people less fortunate than us. People who cannot afford holidays. Charlotte and I build castles encircled by moats which we fill with sea-water collected from rock-pools in our decorated tin buckets. Because of my age, I am not allowed a spade with a cutting-edge. I am not even allowed to borrow Charlotte's, on the grounds that I would cut someone's toes. I have a wooden spade; it is a source of extreme frustration. On the day of the photograph, Charlotte has persuaded Mother and Father into a shop on the esplanade because she wants a yo-yo. The shop is a place of wonder for me. It belongs entirely to holiday time; there is nothing like it in London. It is crammed with comics, sticks of rock, patent medicines for upset tummies and wasp stings, gob-stoppers and sherbet, Wall's snow-fruits, buckets, spades, shrimping-nets, and the sort of postcards that Charlotte and I are forbidden to look at, let alone buy – I know they are to do with bottoms and top bits. . . . Charlotte chooses her yo-yo and a new bucket and a copy of *Beano*. Father takes the comic from her and puts it back on the counter. Mother tells Father that she will pay, so he may leave the shop for the fresher air on the front. Mother snaps her purse open.

'Please, Mother, may I have a shrimping-net?' I ask quietly and politely, as I have been instructed. I really want a spade with a sharp cutting-edge, but I dare not bring that subject up again.

'You most certainly may not!' Mother replies in a low but emphatic voice. 'I don't like you, Antonia, and I don't give presents to little girls I don't like. Little insolent, disobedient, plain girls like you.'

It is when we emerge from this Aladdin's cave and this whispered exchange that we find Father has been accosted by the beach photographer and has had to give in to his suggestion.

All these years later, and only now, do my eyes fill with the tears that dried in the desert of my childhood.

'Yes, thank you, Madge. I did ring. Madame would like a tisane. Bring it to me here and I will take it to her.'

The curtains are drawn across the windows. The room is black dark. Nanny has closed my door. I lie stiff. I am cold. There is a huge gap between my feet and the end of the bed where the night monster will lie curled. I listen: no sound. Not yet. I stop breathing to listen. The wicker chair in front of the long curtains is beginning to creak. She must be there, sitting as still as the stone figures in the garden, her cloak over her head and down to her ankles. I've never seen her face. Perhaps she doesn't have one. I try to scream but no sound comes out. I can't make a scream; I can't move. She's got off the chair, she's coming towards me, she's by the bed, she's bending over me, she's stretching the sheet across my throat, she's going to strangle me . . .

'What in the name of heaven is all this fuss about?'

'The child's an hysteric!'

'Is there nothing she won't do to draw attention to herself?'

'The lady in green. She came to strangle me!'

'I think the solution might be to give her her bedtime snack *before* her bath in future . . .'

'Well, something's got to be done, Nanny, we can't have these commotions night after night, it's most inconvenient. Charlotte never carried on like this at her age. A three-year-old should be more in control. Come along, George, we shall be late for drinks at the Ponsonbys'!'

I tried to remember Father's face but I could call up only its component parts: an almost lipless mouth, a slit no more than that under an ill-fitting door, through which no light can seep but draughts infiltrate; eyes that too closely defended the deep bridge of his aquiline nose; and a low forehead casting the whole in shadow. As I tried hard to fit the parts together, I remembered the photograph in its brown leather frame which had accompanied me to boarding-school. And then I saw Father, thin, tall and costive, staring out unsmilingly, the only sparkle coming from his Sam Browne and cane.

Charlotte was fingering a two-strand string of Mother's perfectly matched pearls at her neck. They must previously have been hanging next to her skin, out of sight under the tent covering her shapelessness, because I had not noticed them. I wondered whether Mother had given them to her or whether, in the circumstances, Charlotte had helped herself. If her intention was to arouse me to comment, she did not succeed. I almost sympathized with her, knowing how keenly she must feel the pleasure of their possession. I could imagine how she would claim to be the proprietor of the house and garden. Charlotte had always needed things. All her concepts derived from external objects – the best being those that were exclusively her own.

Charlotte was unable to distinguish what was intrinsically beautiful from what was fashionable. In the event, she appreciated what was expensive and relied for her taste on Asprey's, Fortnum's and Harrods. Because it had never occurred to her to rebel against Father and Mother and the role they had assigned to her (she had been over-pruned by the parents, her growth had been stunted), she respected the authorities they respected, and obediently celebrated their taste. Most people are lured by what is familiar and like most people Charlotte did not question its rightness. She was to be well rewarded for her slavish adherence. She had been taught to expect that she would be.

'I shall miss Mother when she's gone. I like to have someone to care for. I wanted to nurse her myself. You know that, Antonia. But I just couldn't manage it a day longer. Physically, I mean. Dr Ashburn insisted that Mother needed round-the-clock care. But he doesn't understand that Mother has reverted more and more to speaking German. Of course when *he* visits she's on her best behaviour, but with the nurses it's a horse of a very different colour. I can't so much as leave the house for twenty minutes without there being some sort of upset. "What does Mrs Sinclair mean when she says . . .?" they want to know. And it's always perfectly obvious if only they'd stop to think – she wants to be turned, or she wants a sip of water. I've told them over and over again: "Try a little water, try turning her, try the eau-de-Cologne stick, try wiping her hands on a moist, scented towel. . . ." And I remind them: "She's always cold, whatever the weather. She must have her bedsocks and her hot-water bottle and the little cap I knitted for her head."'

I remembered that she was always cold. How could I have forgotten? She burrowed her way into my being like a tapeworm, and I had neither obliterated her nor flushed her out. Merely repressed her. Why, I wondered, were people absolved from soul murder? She had pollarded me emotionally. Mother's single sentence, uttered quietly so that no one else would hear what she dared to confide to her small daughter, had been responsible for the complex of feeling I had carried with me ever since: the succubus. 'I don't like you . . . I don't give presents to little girls I don't like.'

'Doesn't your mother give you presents?'

It is my birthday. I am standing in the queue with the rest of my class outside the dining-room before lunch. The post is being distributed. Miss Frobisher, the assistant head, stands behind a table on which there are piles of letters and parcels. She examines each and announces: 'Jane, you have a parcel from your grandmother in Sussex. Lucy, you have a letter from your father. Oh, I see that he's been posted overseas! Antonia, you have a birthday card from your Uncle Walter and one from Nanny. You lucky girl!'

'Doesn't your mother write to you on your birthday?' One of my class interrogates me as we file into the dining-room. 'Doesn't anyone give you presents? Or can't they afford to?'

'My parents save my presents for when I get home,' I lie. I lie not out of a sense of family loyalty – so dear to Father, Mother and Charlotte – but out of shame. I did not know which was less humiliating: to be poor or unconsidered. Later, when I am alone, I weep. I often weep when I am alone, but never for so long and so desperately as on my birthday.

'I said I wanted Charlotte to bring me my tisane!' Mother whined.

'Charlotte's just slipped out to the shops to find you some muscats.'

'I don't like her to leave me. Not now.'

'But *I'm* here!'

'It's not the same!'

'Why send the child to school at all?' Walter is addressing my outraged father and my speechless mother. 'Why not keep her

with you, educate her yourselves? Learning to recognize the flags
of the world and repeat *Hiawatha* by heart, learning the dates of
the arrivals and departures of the kings and queens of England,
learning her tables, learning to swim faster and jump higher than
other little girls of her age – it's really not the same as acquiring
knowledge, George.' Walter is confronting Father. 'Is it, Lisa?'
Walter is confronting Mother. Then, turning to me: 'Knowledge
is something you will eventually acquire at my side!' I am uncom-
fortably confused. I know that Father won't say anything to contra-
dict Walter. He never does. Merely ignores him. 'You said that all
a decent woman needs to know is how to waltz and play the piano,
George. Surely Antonia can be taught both at home?'

Father has his head down, sorting through music scores. He
always takes a selection of piano music when he is posted to a new
billet. He says that it softens the blow. I approach his side and ask
him where he is being sent this time.

'It's a secret, Antonia, I can't tell you and I can't tell Mother. All
I'm allowed to say is "somewhere in Britain". "Careless talk costs
lives", you know.'

Father and Walter rarely exchange words. If they do want to say
something to one another, one looks towards the other and then
the other looks away. They often utter long speeches in each
other's direction, uninterrupted and unacknowledged. Walter is
waiting for Father to say something about my education, but
Father says nothing. He leaves the room.

'One day, my little one, when school has done its worst to lay
you low, and stuff your head with the dregs of things, I shall come
along and serve you the vintages.'

As is so often the case, I do not really understand what Walter is
saying, but I am confident that what he means is that he has
something nice in store for me when I am older. And I know that
he will keep his word. He always does. Lovely treats! The zoo, the
pantomime, concerts at the Queen's Hall, little presents and big
presents – 'I will not have you spending large sums of money on
the child!' – and secrets. 'You do so spoil Antonia!'

Father has returned to the drawing-room. He has forgotten
something, I suppose. He has changed into uniform. 'Kukky', I
call it, and it does look ugly and unfriendly next to Walter's suit.
Walter's suit also comes from Savile Row, but it is dark grey and
chalk-striped. I know the name of the tailor: Mr Hawkes. And I

know something that Father does not and must not know. It is to do with the bill for Walter's suit. Father spreads his broad, hairy hands on the piano-lid and cracks his knuckles. I hate that sound. He often makes it when he is cross. Walter has thin, hairless hands with tapered fingers and lovely clean nails, and he never makes noises with them. Father is in one of his moods. He is spitting bullets, Mother says. Walter has given up talking to Father and is by the window, looking out over the porch and the garden furniture towards the orchard. He says we are in for some very fine weather and a great fruit harvest. But all around Father there is crossness.

'Of course she'll go back to school. I went away at her age. Actually, I was younger. Seven. That's the way we do things in England. Knock her into shape. The child's going to have to learn to conform.'

Only Walter ever visited me at school. He alone made the wearisome journey from wherever he was billeted to Northumberland.

'Do you think Mother and Father will ever come up to see me? I do wish they would. All the other parents come.'

Walter says that travel is difficult in wartime.

'Why doesn't Mother call me darling, like other mothers call their daughters?'

'It's just not her way. But I call you my darling and my *Liebchen*, don't I? Isn't that enough for you?'

I do not tell Walter that it is not enough. I do not like to.

'Helen's mother sits Helen on her lap and kisses her. She's not a baby. I've seen her. I like that. I don't like having a nanny. Helen didn't have a nanny. Phoebe didn't have a nanny. Their mothers always took care of them.'

'Don't think about such things, *Liebchen*. You've got me. Helen and Phoebe don't have a Walter, do they? You'll always have me.'

I start to explain to Walter that there are lots of people to be 'not-parents' but only two to be parents, and mine are neither one thing nor the other. But we are approaching the Swan Inn and Walter interrupts to tell me that he has organized a very special treat. He has brought up a big piece of veal and Chef is going to prepare it with egg and breadcrumbs and we are going to have a Wiener schnitzel. 'And there'll be ice-cream galore!'

Unable to control me, my parents had no interest in me.

'You were completely and utterly uncontrollable as a child! *Unerhört.*' Mother's recollections have gathered force once again. 'Your father used to ask you repeatedly whether it wouldn't be easier to conform. But the idea never appealed to you then and I don't imagine it does now. None of my friends' daughters are archaeologists. And how is it that you are not married? I hope there's nothing peculiar about you, Antonia.'

Because I never confided in Mother, and because I remained unmarried, on the rare occasions when I had spoken to her in the past she had managed always to convey to me her suspicions that my general lack of conformity may have extended to sexual licence. She would accuse me of promiscuity: 'Don't expect me to provide a white wedding for you. It would be most inappropriate!' Or she would suggest, darkly, that I was 'peculiar'.

'It's certainly not that I'm homosexual, Mother,' I told her.

'How dare you use that word in this house!' And she promptly drew the covers over her head and started to weep. 'Where's Walter? Where's Walter? Why doesn't Walter come to see me?' *Valter, Valter, Valter.*

'Walter's dead, Mother. He's been dead for years.'

'You wicked, wicked girl!'

Did Mother believe I was lying to her? Or did she feel that I was stating a truth so distasteful that it should be kept from her? Would she, in her enfeebled state of mind, recall that when I was a child either transgression would have led her and Father to threaten me with the reformatory? In my family life it was always five minutes before a pogrom.

I am able to walk, but not so far as the park and round the lake and back to the house. For this reason, Nanny pushes the pram and I jump in for the return journey when I am exhausted. It is a lovely feeling rolling along the velvet-smooth paths between the shrubs and over the bridge and along the tow-path by the canal, where the ducks and the swan nest. But the lovely feeling is always spoilt for me when I remember we are going to pass the keeper's lodge. I do wish Nanny didn't like the park keeper. I hide under the pram cover.

'Nanny Sinclair!' I hear him calling. 'Wait!' And now I can hear his huge boots crunching up the path like big dogs crunch their biscuits. He is going to push his arm under my pram cover and catch one of my legs and hold on to it and pretend he's found one of the park's squirrels.

I scream. I sit bolt upright and face the man in the black uniform with the silver buttons.

'And how many squirrels have you stolen today, little girl?'

'None! None!' I am screaming and I am horribly frightened.

'It's only Mr Batch, the park keeper, having a joke,' Nanny tries to reassure me.

But Mr Batch looks very much like a policeman to me, and it is a policeman who would be called to take me off to the reformatory.

Father has told me that disobedient, untruthful, uncontrollable children are taken away from their parents by policemen in big black vans and shut up in reformatories that are a bit like army barracks but more like prisons for thieves and murderers. Naughty children have to stay in these places until they have learnt to be good, and that can take a very long time with some children, so it's better not to be sent there in the first place. Father has taken me in the car and shown me one of these places from the outside: a huge building, larger than a railway station, grey, shut up behind a tall wall that nobody could possibly climb over.

'That's the place. That's the reformatory where they'd shut you up!' he tells me.

He stood me on the pavement opposite the building so that I could see the whole horrible place clearly. It's very, very big. It has tiny windows with bars. It has no doors that I can see: no way to get out. Father says that to get out they have to cut open the wall, and they hardly ever do that. I wet my knickers.

And now it comes back to me. . . . The bus-conductor made me feel I hadn't paid my fare. The milkman made me feel I'd stolen from his float. The road sweeper and the dustman made me feel responsible for their arduous toil.

Mother is sitting on the sofa in the drawing-room surrounded by eight other women all dressed for luncheon. They are wearing hats with veils and lots of jewellery. They have pads of paper on their laps and gold fountain-pens in their hands. There is an expensive smell.

'But we don't want *Ost-Juden* pouring into this country.' One of the women sounds very sure about this. 'There must be plenty of nice, professional men – even artists – who need to be saved. You must make it clear, Lisa, it's such men we are interested in.'

I am peering through the crack in the unclosed door. Nanny sees me and drags me off, knowing that my presence is always greeted as an intrusion. I do not understand what is meant by *Ost-Juden* and when I ask Nanny she doesn't know either. It is many years later that I discover that Mother and her committee operated a caste system in their charity work – rather like Hitler.

'Why oh why are you shut up in your room on such a glorious day?' Walter is talking to me from behind my locked bedroom door. ' *"Was hat man dir, du armes Kind, getan?"* '

'Mother says I've been insolent. I'm being punished.'

I hear Walter walking to the top of the stairs. He calls out over the banisters: 'Lisa, what's all this about?' I can't hear what she says but I hear Walter say: 'Don't be so absurd. Let the child out!'

Now I hear Mother's footsteps on the stairs.

'You always take her side. You don't mind at all that she's rude to me. You're far too soft with her. She's got to learn, you know.'

Mother is speaking German, in the funny voice she uses when she talks to Walter and thinks no one is around to hear. I know that when she speaks this way Walter can usually get whatever he wants out of her. She seems, mostly, to like to please Walter, which is funny because she almost never seems to want to please Father. And while I am thinking these thoughts, Mother gives Walter the key to my room and he opens my door.

'Why are you so naughty, *Liebchen*?' Walter asks me.

'I can't help it,' I explain. 'It's the night creature. He lives in the cupboard over there where I keep my shoes and he gets right up into the toes, and when I put my shoes on he worms his way up my legs and into my tummy and keeps me naughty. He likes naughtiness and naughty people. He said so!'

31

'Oh, so that's it!' I am so glad Walter understands. 'I don't imagine Lisa and George know about the night creature and I'm not sure if they did that they'd understand, so we'd better keep him a secret.' Walter has picked me up and put me on his knee. 'Your mother and father have no time at all for naughty little girls.' I wonder whether Walter is trying to explain to me why they punish me. 'They only like good little girls. Good girls are girls who are no trouble to their parents, who do as they are told and don't answer back. You answer back, don't you? In England that's called being insolent. Parents don't like being questioned.' Walter is saying each thing slowly, looking at me to see if I'm listening. 'And your father's an officer, someone who never allows his soldiers to question him, even if the soldier has something quite sensible to suggest. In England, soldiers, servants and children have been invented to make parents and officers feel big and strong and always in the right.' Now Walter is jogging me up and down on his knees and is laughing so I know I can laugh too. Then he says something I don't really understand about the English in Africa and India.

I do not remember the transgression for which I received the most memorable thrashing. It cannot have been as heinous as the punishment proved fateful. At the time, I knew that the pain to my bottom would pass, but I knew too that I should always remain puzzled by the effect my beating had on Mother and Father.

I am in Father's dressing-room. I have been brought along by Nanny, who is carrying my Mason Pearson hairbrush. There is nothing unusual about Nanny taking me into Father's dressing-room. Sometimes he asks Nanny to bring me along if he wants to have a talk with me. Sometimes Mother does my hair there.
'You may leave, Nanny.'
Now I know, from the icy way Father speaks to Nanny, that something is wrong. Mother is standing by Father's side. She waits until Nanny has shut the door behind her before she grabs hold of the collar of my dress and drags me across the room into the corner. She shakes me. 'Pull down your knickers!' she orders.
'Why . . .?'

'Because I say so!'

I try, but with Mother standing over me, frightening me, I can't get my knickers over my shoes. Mother is tapping her toe impatiently on the floor by my side. She wants me to be quick. At last I manage to pull my knickers off and Mother seizes them and throws them right across the room into the far corner. She catches hold of me and chucks me over Father's lap. My head is hanging over his legs, close to the floor. Mother's legs are very close. I can see that she is still tapping her toe on the carpet. Father thrashes my bottom again and again with the back of my hairbrush. My bottom is stinging. I scream. I am hurt, badly. Most of all, I am frightened. What will happen next? Will this ever stop? I am hot and cold at once and I want to go to the lavatory.

'Get off!' Father shouts, but I can't move. He opens his legs and I fall between them on to the floor. Mother shouts at me to go and put on my knickers. I crawl to the far corner of the room, but my fingers won't work and I can't get my knickers on over my shoes. I look up, desperately. I need help. Mother and Father are standing facing one another, so close they look like a single person. I cannot remember ever having seen them locked together like this before. Although I am very surprised, I am crying loudly and I am still shaking. I fall back on my bottom but it hurts so badly I get to my knees and crouch.

'Mother! Mother! Help me!'

But she ignores me. I do not even try to enlist Father's help. I think how strangely they are behaving. They seem to be quite deaf. I have often been beaten, pinched and kicked, but I have never seen Mother in Father's arms. I have never seen Mother cover Father's face with kisses. I have never before heard Father murmur Mother's name – Lisa! Lisa! – so lovingly.

Mother was sobbing under the bedclothes. 'Walter! Walter!'

I am three. I am very pleased with the way Nanny has dressed me. I am wearing a smocked Liberty print dress that I am fond of and a panama bonnet, on the brim of which is attached a posy of artificial daisies, violets and stalks of wheat. I am feeling very happy. Mother, Father, Walter and I (I do not remember if

Charlotte was present) are in the garden of a country hotel with a big hill behind it. It is Sunday. We are seated at a table overlooking the river. I am blowing bubbles through my straw into my lemonade and I have not been ordered to stop. The grown-ups are talking to each other and seem to be friends. A waiter is coming towards us across the lawn. He tells Father that our table is ready for luncheon. I take my paper bag to the water's edge and throw the bread to the ducks. The adults start walking towards the hotel terrace.

'Antonia! Come along!' It is Walter calling, and I look up. 'Come on. It's lunchtime for us, too!' I immediately run to him and he catches me up in his arms and kisses me. '*Liebchen! Liebchen!*' he repeats. Suddenly, there is confusion. The happiness stops. Everything is spoilt now because Mother is crying and Father has stomped off.

'*I* am your *Liebchen!*' Mother is wailing. '*I* am your *Liebchen*! And don't you forget it!' she adds, furiously. She hits Walter's arm. But worst of all, Walter has put me down and dropped my hand.

'Charlotte is a person of absolute integrity.' Mother has dried her eyes and chosen another topic. She conveyed this piece of character analysis with a display of confidential certainty. 'She never lied to us. She was never disobedient,' she added.

This memory enlivened Mother and she continued to comfort herself with a comparison of her two daughters. All models of behaviour held out to me to admire were neither ridiculous or disgusting. They always had been. But the word 'integrity' held a particularly memorable position in the canon of Mother's preferences. She had never consulted a dictionary. For her, integrity was a euphemism for a woman's sexual inviolability. There was never much she admired in women, but virgins and frigid females always had the edge on others. I was not surprised about Charlotte, but I did feel momentary pity for her.

However, I thought, it was as well that Mother admired and complimented Charlotte for her unspectacular life, led almost exclusively in the service of herself. I did not imagine that Mother loved Charlotte, I had no evidence that she was capable of such warmth and softness as mere fondness would entail, but, God knows, she loved herself and knew what was best for her.

'And Charlotte always had such charming friends. *Entzückend!*' The memory of Charlotte's tendency to choose 'suitable' company aroused Mother to a sickly sweetness. My friends were invariably labelled 'common'. 'Do you remember Colonel Frobisher's wife and their daughter, Victoria?'

'Mrs Frobisher, how very nice to hear your voice. Yes, *I* prefer the Berkeley for luncheon. I thought Victoria looked quite lovely. Now, about the ball. . . .' Mother talks to Mrs Frobisher at length. She covers every one of her preferred topics.

'Did Mrs Frobisher remark on me, Mother?' I inquire anxiously.

'What an extraordinary idea! Why should she have?'

Mother has a habit of talking about me on the telephone so that I can *just* hear some of what she is saying. This makes me feel cold inside and very unhappy and anxious but I cannot resist hanging around and listening.

'Listeners never did hear any good of themselves,' she tells me when she finds me crying behind the door. Mother has the monopoly of righteousness.

'But, Mother, I don't lie to you. Ever,' I object, having just overheard her say: 'I can't find my locket, you know the one, I'm sure, the little enamel heart Papa bought in Vienna that time . . . my lipstick . . . the gold propelling pencil from my diary. . . . Of course we all know who borrows these items. My dear Marjorie, I just don't know what to do with the child. She's a thief and a liar. It's a most frightful cross to bear. George will give her a thrashing when he comes in. . . .'

I look at Mother's mouth. It's puffy with mocking and cutting words. If I were to clap my hands over her cheeks they'd all come tumbling out: like sick. They'd all be about me! They'd all be lies!

I was neither a thief nor a liar. In fact, I was an almost pathologically honest child. I say 'pathologically' advisedly (incalculable harm was done to my heart by branding it with distrust), for there were many occasions on which it would have been more prudent for me to have lied to my parents than to have told the truth. I should have avoided both their displeasure and their abuse. Father used to leave his small change on the desk in his dressing-room overnight. I was repeatedly accused of taking coins from this little pile. Despite the fact that my parents were hardly liberal with pocket-money, I never helped myself to so much as a threepenny piece.

I hated being lied about, being disbelieved and misquoted, but not once did I find the courage to tell those listening to my parents' own falsehoods that I was nothing like the child reported to them. I knew from my earliest days that it was not from want of perception that Mother lied. It was something she did naturally and by preference from an overflowing excess of mendacity.

One day I heard a very different sort of exchange. Mother was addressing Uncle Harold, telling him that I was a 'throw-back', that my peculiar imagination and my uncontrollable emotions were a legacy from the ghetto. 'Certainly not the avenue!' She was speaking in a low voice so that the servants would not hear and the tone of her voice was tinged with something unfamiliar. Instead of lashing out against me, she was expressing herself thoughtfully.

'It's most peculiar how this child has developed. Not at all as one might have expected, given Charlotte's example. And school's not helped. She's foreign to both George and me. I think she should be baptized. A dose of the Church of England might improve her. And if it doesn't, it will at least help her in the husband stakes.'

Later, I remonstrated with Mother: 'You are a Jew, Mother, and I am your child!' Without really understanding why I felt so strongly about my heritage being wrested from me, I insisted fiercely that I would never be baptized, never worship in church.

'If you say so,' Mother said, rather quietly for her, settling nothing but seeming, slightly, to be on the retreat, and she left the room.

'No! Certainly not! I'm not having Nanny spend her time entertaining your so-called friends. She's got quite enough on her hands without running after Helen.'

'But Mother, I go to Helen's all the time!'

'Be that as it may. It's for Helen's mother to decide. And where is the watch Granny Sinclair left you?' Mother has grabbed my wrist, the one on which my watch should properly be strapped. I look down at my shoes. Despite the seriousness of what is going on (or perhaps because of it), I notice that they are rather small for me and my big toes have thrown them out of shape. 'Look at me when I'm talking to you!' My right hand is in the pocket of my dress, my fingers are wound tightly round a tiny tin – a sample of Huntley and Palmer's cheese biscuits – which I have swapped with Helen for my gold watch. I am passionately fond of the toy grocer's shop that Walter has given me. I am collecting things for it. 'If you don't tell me at once where your watch is, I shall telephone your father. I shall shut you in the broom cupboard for the whole day until he comes home to give you a good thrashing.'

I run into the garden and hide in the currant hedge. Eventually, more humiliated than I have ever been, I am forced to tell Helen that I have to swap back.

'One of your troubles is that you have no proper sense of values.' I am told this both by Mother and by Father. For several days I find I am deaf in one ear – on the side of my face that Father swiped.

'I thought it perfectly sweet of Victoria. *Süss.* Do you know what? She's such a busy young woman but she dropped everything to come round and see me. She brought me the most beautiful flowers from Moyses Stevens. . . . And what am I to her? Just a poor old woman, a friend of her mother's. . . . *Natürlich* she did this little errand of mercy for Charlotte. I understand that. I haven't noticed any of *your* fine friends dropping anything on my account. But then you hardly set them an example, do you? You were born selfish, d'you know that? Born selfish. I don't know where you got it from. Not from your father or me. I think Walter was very much to blame. He spoilt you.'

'There's nothing to argue about. You will not be going to the pantomime and that's that. You've been rude to your mother and you must be punished.'

It seems a lifetime that I have been looking forward to this treat. Walter and *Cinderella* have occupied my thoughts by day and my dreams by night. To be alone with Walter at the Theatre Royal, Drury Lane! And now I'm going to be shut in my room instead.

'But what will Walter say? He's got the tickets and everything.'

'Walter will say that he's very disappointed in you and he'll take another little girl.'

Walter says nothing of the sort. He searches me out, and with his arms tightly about me he draws me into the nursery and sits me down by his side in front of the hissing gas fire. He takes two oranges, and into the top of each he pushes a lump of sugar. We sit side by side, sucking juice from the oranges through the sugar. Walter makes a loud noise doing this and encourages me to do likewise. Eventually, when I am calm, he says: 'Don't worry, little one, there are many Christmases to come.'

'But you've bought the tickets . . .' I complain anxiously.

He fishes in his pocket and draws out an envelope from which he extracts two tickets. He tears them up in front of my eyes. 'You know, *Liebchen*, I'd never take anyone else. You and I will go a little later in the season, when all this is forgotten about. Or next year.'

'Next year!' I wail. He might just as well have said, in a future life. . . . Despite all attempts to stop my sobs, they erupt every few seconds.

Walter wipes his mouth and mine on a lovely soft, silk handkerchief, smelling of something delicious I associate only with him. He gathers me up and settles me by his side on the nursery sofa. He takes up a book that is lying on the table: '"Oh, don't go on like that," cried the poor Queen, wringing her hands in despair. "Consider what a great girl you are. Consider what a long way you've come today. Consider what o'clock it is. Consider anything, only don't cry."' And he hugs me and he kisses me. 'Don't worry, *Liebchen*. And always remember this: There is nothing to be afraid of.'

Don't worry, *Liebchen*. There is nothing to be afraid of. It might have been our signature tune.

It is summer. Walter and I are walking along the lavender path, admiring the industrious bees as they explore every floret of every flower on every stalk. Walter is talking to me as if I were a grown-up. I am feeling very proud.

'When you're older, you'll discover that the English are obsessed with sex.' He stops by the pool and we watch together as the goldfish dart. 'We would all be a deal happier if our lives were as uncomplicated as theirs.' He indicates that we are going to sit on the steps of the summer-house. I wonder whether Walter is expecting me to say something in reply, or to ask a question, but I can't think of anything to say about sex or goldfish. And while I think about this failure on my part, Walter goes on: 'That's because they're so bad at love. The English, I mean. The goldfish are fine at it.'

I am confused now. I am sure Walter is telling me something important that I should understand. But I don't. I start thinking about Father: he *is* very bad at love. Then about Mother: she's very bad at love but she's not English. Were Mother or Father any good at sex, whatever that is? Should I ask Walter? I decide not to. I remember hearing Mother tell Walter: 'In this house we do not discuss religion, politics or sex.' She sounded very firm about it. I expect she meant in the garden, too.

'And I had a hip operation. It was agony.'
I sense the imminence of tears.

'How did you break your arm, little girl?'
'I fell,' I lie. But I keep my head down.
'How did you come by this burn?'
'I brushed against the fire.'
'How did you get these bruises?'
'I bumped into . . . I fell. . . .'

It was many years later that I read Bettelheim and recognized the 'terrible silence of children who are forced to endure the unendurable'.

'Charlotte said she told you about my operation. Why didn't you visit me in hospital?'
I had had too much to bear, too many reproaches, too much

contempt, too many beatings, that's why. I'd learnt how to switch off: not to experience. You interpret that as my being cold. It was my defence. Would you have put up with ridicule?

'Will you collect me from Helen's party, Mummy?'
'Certainly not! Nanny will collect you, as usual.'
'But other children's mothers. . . .'

'I've never been able to understand your complete lack of consideration for me, Antonia.'
This puzzle, which Mother had spent my lifetime trying to unravel, so tired her that she dropped off to sleep. I watched her. Her mouth fell open and her breathing became uneven and seemed to emerge with difficulty, through fluid. Time passed.

'This is for you, Father. I made it.'
'What on earth's it supposed to be?' Father mumbles under his breath but quite loud enough for me to hear. He is turning my horse this way and that in his hand. He is examining my horse's belly, its head, its mane and tail.
'It's a horse, Father, like the ones at the barracks.'
'It doesn't much look like one,' he remarks.
Mother is coming into the room. 'You don't use your eyes, child,' she says, picking up my horse. 'Really!' she laughs.
Later in the day I hear her telling Nanny that the best place for Antonia's works of art is the back of the pantry cupboard for the time being 'until she forgets it and we can throw it out'.
Nothing I can do pleases Mother or Father. Good marks are expected, bad ones rebuked. They never say: 'How lovely, darling!' They don't like me as I am but having got me they want to mould me to a more pleasing design. Theirs.

'Have your table manners improved? I always wished. . . .'
I had been leafing through a copy of *Country Life* while Mother slept uneasily and I was not expecting her to waken yet, far less to find that she was preoccupied by memories of my table manners.

'They were dreadful when you were a child. *Schrecklich*. You ate with your mouth wide open. You stretched across the table, never waiting to be passed the condiments. And if you didn't like what had been prepared for you, you refused to swallow it. You would store it in lumps in your cheek for hours on end. *Natürlich* Nanny never let you leave food on your plate. Quite rightly, she insisted that you ate up whatever you were served.'

I remembered those lumps of unwanted, disgusting food I stored in my cheek, unable to swallow them and not allowed from the table until I had. Did people these days, I wondered, torture their children like that?

'No, Mother, I don't imagine you would think my table manners have improved. I still don't eat grapes with a fork.' God almighty, the old woman was dying and she was still obsessed with trivialities. 'Have you heard, Mother, there's been an earthquake in China? A million Chinese are feared dead.' Needless to say, there had been no such earthquake.

'China is vastly overpopulated,' was Mother's considered response. 'What happened to that little friend of yours, Helen? A funny child. Her mother was rather – how shall I put it? – odd.'

'Helen's mummy calls her "darling" and hugs and kisses her. So does her daddy. You don't do that to me, do you?'

Mother leaves the room quickly. 'Nanny! Give the child an early bath, will you?' she calls over her shoulder.

'Helen joined Voluntary Service Overseas. She's in India, arranging for water to be piped to people who've never had it. Mrs Armstrong is well. She's still living in the Chilterns with her animals. I see her quite often. I go down for weekends.'

'Now, I'm warning you. Don't you make a scene. Your are not keeping that puppy. I couldn't countenance such a thing! I shall ring Mrs Armstrong right away and tell her that she had no business imposing this animal on us.'

'But Mother, please. . . . Please let me keep him. I love Patch.'

'Love! Love! What do you know about love?'

'Didn't you want to be a vet when you were a child? A most unwholesome occupation.'

'So you said at the time. And I remember how you couldn't imagine why I should want a profession at all, why I wanted to be anything but a wife and mother, like you. But then you did rather spoil it by saying that you thought I'd find it difficult to persuade anyone to marry me, and I ought to do a secretarial course, just in case.'

'And wasn't I quite right?'

'No, Mother, you were quite confused and you were wrong.'

A silence ensued. Mother would have called me 'insolent' had she not been a cat's whisker from death. She was not accustomed to dealing with contention, so she sighed deeply instead. In the silence I recalled Walter telling me that Mother had in all seriousness admitted to him that she had *once* been wrong, but that she could never remember what about or when.

'On the one hand you used to accuse me of promiscuity and on the other tell me that I was too plain to attract a man.'

'I'm sure I never said such things. Indeed I always made a point of telling you that you had nice eyes and skin. But it does rather look as if you've missed the boat, as the English say. But what I always say is this: "A good name is rather to be chosen than great riches." You do have a good name?' she inquired darkly – and, no doubt, with her mind on 'integrity'.

'"Go to the ant, thou sluggard; consider her ways and be wise." You are so lazy, child!'

Mother is surveying me from the *chaise-longue* in her dressing-room. She wishes to give the impression that she views me from a vantage-point she shares with God. She is relaxing. She has told me to ring the bell for her afternoon tea, and when the maid arrives with the tray, tells her to fetch Nanny.

'Nanny, the child is doing nothing. I don't want her laziness encouraged. From now on she's to clean the nursery herself. And I mean by that, the floor, the table, the toy cupboard – everything. Tell Mrs Rudge she's not to touch that room in future. And I want you to see that she does it properly. She's eight now, and she's got to learn that things don't get done by themselves.'

Mother always rests on the *chaise* in the afternoon. I am old enough to know the routines of the house now. I know, for example, that this morning she will have given Cook the orders, telephoned the grocer and done the flowers that Mr Henderson will have cut and left in the pantry for her to arrange. And she will have written some letters.

'"He that loveth pleasure shall be a poor man,"' she quotes. 'You are going to have to learn to pay your way in life, Antonia.'

I look at Mother, lying in her silk kimono – all pink and wobbly – against velvet upholstery.

'But, Mother, *you* don't do anything!'

'How dare you! You insolent child! You're asking for a thrashing!'

Her ways are far from pleasantness; her paths are far from peace. . . .

'Do you remember, Mother, how Walter taught me that *"Ein unnutz Leben ist ein früher Tod"*?'

Mother found it possible to ignore my question. She knew the power of silence, but not its implication. Indeed, it was from Mother that I had learnt the technique and acquired the knowledge of its source: aggression. 'A useless life is an early death,' Walter used to repeat. All through my childhood I watched Mother inert, killing time, dressing for the theatre, for dinner, finding excuses for not doing this and that, and revelling in the certainty that she could always pay someone to do for her what she did not wish to do for herself. 'I find people love to be asked to do things for me,' she would sigh. 'I suppose it is that everyone requires to feel needed, to have some sort of purpose. . . .'

The deposits in her unconscious lent her utterances a sort of piety.

'I never gave in. I kept up my charity work at the hospital even after my hip operation. It was only at Dr Ashburn's insistence that I stopped. He said to me: "Frankly, Mrs Sinclair, you really must not exhaust yourself on behalf of others. You are just not strong enough."' Mother's voice rang out loud and clear.

Mother does not drive. Every week, on a Wednesday, a hire car arrives at the house to take her to the East End, to a geriatric hospital, a ward of which is funded by the Society of Ethical Monotheists to which Mother belongs. On our journeys to and from the hospital Mother takes the opportunity to remind me of the dictates of the Bible. She instructs me on the benefits of 'working willingly with my hands', 'rising when it is yet night' (*'Morgenstunde hat Gold in Munde'*), 'planting a vineyard' (something I make a note to discuss with Mr Henderson when we get home), and 'finding on my tongue a teaching of kindness'. I do not remind Mother about 'the bread of idleness'.

For these occasions Mother has made 'suitable outfits'. They are run up by a needy dressmaker in West Hampstead. Mother chooses suits in sombre colours and inexpensive cloth, and with these garments fabric, not leather, gloves and untrimmed hats. She spends up to two hours at the bedsides of poor, sick co-religionists who, like her, are strangers in England. During the school holidays she insists that I accompany her. I hate these visits; all the patients are very old (and dying) and the women have whiskers on their chins and often spittle at the corners of their mouths. The men are, if anything, more disgusting. I am instructed by Mother to stand quite still by the side of the beds so that the deafest among the patients can hear what I must say to them. There is always a nasty smell. Over and over I am asked how old I am and whether I like school. I am told that I have a beautiful, kind mummy and am lucky to have been born in England and to have plenty of money.

When we leave the Isaac Levy Ward for Destitute Jews, Matron accompanies us down the stairs to the steps that lead to the Mile End Road. As we reach the pavement, beggars approach Mother. Mother ignores them as she sweeps towards the car, but I can't help noticing that the chauffeur has his hand in his trouser pocket and, as soon as he has closed the rear car door after Mother and seen me into the front seat, he gives his loose change to the poor old men.

'The most important alms we have to give the poor is the reassurance that in the eyes of God all men are equal,' Mother tells me.

'Have you learnt to compromise?'

'I don't think so, Mother,' I say sweetly, adding that because something lies between what I see as ideal and what others see as impossible, I do not feel I should meet them half-way.

'It can't make you very popular.'

'No, you're quite right. It doesn't.'

I am seven. I am playing in the nursery with Mr Bear when suddenly I am disturbed by a loud commotion: shrieks are rising from the floor below and furniture is being hurled about. I hurry to the landing.

'Bitch. Criminal. Insolent bloody child!' Mother is yelling these words at Father. She is running up and down the landing, throwing underwear and cosmetics this way and that over the banisters. Drawers from her chest of drawers are lying on the landing. 'I've really had enough! She'll have to go!'

Go? Where? I know that 'she' is me. I am seized with the urgent need to get to the lavatory but instead I run and hide behind the nursery curtains. It's no good. I can hear Father's steps. He is running along the corridor.

'Antonia! Antonia! Where are you? Come out AT ONCE!'

There is no point in hiding, he'll find me. . . . I unwrap myself from the curtains. I hold my arm across my face in a gesture of protection to ward off the inevitable blows. Father hurls himself at me, catches me by both my arms, lifts me some inches off the ground and plonks me down rigid, knowing that I shall surely freeze with fright. He slaps my face, once, twice, three times. I stop counting. 'If this doesn't do you any good and make you understand, I don't know what will!' Now he is hitting my legs. He is puce with rage. 'This is a fine thing!'

'What is?' I ask in all innocence.

'Don't give me that!' And he pulls my arms this way and that. 'You know perfectly well,' he assures me, 'and you're coming downstairs with me at once to face the music, to see the damage you've done. You're going to get down on your knees to your mother and beg for her mercy. You'll need to. She wants to kill you. And you're going to have to do one hell of a lot of explaining to me.'

The pain Father inflicted on me that day was clearly regarded by him as a purifier. His abuse of me, like Mother's, had a ritualistic quality.

Father drags me down to Mother's dressing-room, where Mother is now seated on her *chaise* with a pile of clothes on her lap. I can see that some of her dresses are covered with ink-stains, while others appear to have been ripped to pieces. I am shown every garment, one by one. I am asked why I did such a thing.

'I didn't!' I tell them, because I hadn't.

'Not satisfied by being a wicked vandal, she's a liar too. Deal with her, George! You're a man – deal with her!'

I know what dealing with me involves and I try to run out of the room, but Father catches me and starts hitting out at me in a wild way. He is in a temper, the worst I have seen. I start to shake but am rooted to the spot. He gets me round the legs and face. He slaps my face with the palm of his hand and, not wanting to waste energy and opportunity, with the back of his hand before replacing it along the seam of his trouser leg. All the time he hangs on to my other arm, which he pinches.

'I didn't do it! I didn't do it!' I am crying. 'Really, I didn't do it!' But I know that I shall not be believed.

'Liar! I've always hated that child!' Mother is sobbing convulsively over her ruined wardrobe. 'I shall have to go through all those fittings again . . . so fatiguing!' she complains. 'And I'll never be able to track down those lovely fabrics . . . or those old buttons. . . .'

It emerges that not only is the ruined fabric hand-woven but the smashed buttons are antique.

'This time you did a really fine job. A fine job!' Father is shaking his head ominously. He has exhausted his temper and is slumped on a chair. 'Where, may I ask, did you get the scissors for this? How did you smash the buttons? Did you take ink from my study? Answer me. I am waiting.' But he sounds defeated already.

'I didn't do it, Father. I promise. I didn't do it.'

'You're going to have to be put away. I've just about had enough of all this. You're not normal. You can't be trusted with anything.'

When Father flings me back into the nursery and locks me in, I am shaking uncontrollably. My nose is bleeding, my legs are bruised and my knickers are wet through. 'Lie down, face down!' he shouts. Later, I understood that to prostrate oneself was to make a sign of death.

I know that of all the things belonging to Mother, she prizes her clothes most dearly. I wonder who did that to her dresses, coats and suits. Poor Mother! It's a terrible thing to have happened. Who could have done it? I approach my bed and find Mr Bear. 'I didn't do it, you know I didn't do it, don't you?'

I am in disgrace. No one – not Cook, Nanny, Charlotte or Mrs Rudge the charwoman, or any of the maids – is allowed to speak to me. Nanny cuts my plaits off ('Let that be a lesson to you, little Miss') and brings me my meals on a tray: bread, milk and greens. No, I may not go into the garden. Worst of all, Walter is not allowed to see me.

When, eventually, Father unlocks the nursery door, he tells me that since I am not a normal child, I may be a sick child and I am going to be taken to a doctor. I do not feel ill, exactly, just sore and bruised from Father's hits and punches. Where he stood on my foot it's very painful and there's a blue-black bruise.

'Is the doctor in the reformatory?'

Father does not answer me.

The doctor is in a house in Harley Street. A hire car calls to take Mother and me there. A lady wearing a pink jumper and a row of pearls opens the door and shows us into a room where there are lots of silent, seated people and a large round table on which the lady has dealt magazines, like playing-cards, in little piles. Mother says I am not to touch. I am to sit up straight with my hands in my lap and on no account am I to speak. Mother has had Nanny dress me in my navy coat with the white velvet collar, long white leggings and black patent pumps. Usually, when I am dressed like this, it's for something nice with Walter: the pantomime or tea at Madame Sagne's. I have been forbidden to bring Mr Bear.

'The doctor can see you now.'

Another lady, this one in a white overall and a sort of white crown on her hair, walks in front of Mother and me and opens the door to an oddly dark room. I can just make out a funny little man with spectacles sitting behind a desk. He stands up but doesn't seem any taller. He extends his arm over the desk to shake Mother's hand.

'Lisa, my dear, how very good to see you! How are you these days? You're looking wonderful! Still Miss Baden-Baden. . . ? I know, it's difficult to come to terms. . . .' He speaks to Mother in German and I do not understand every word. 'Now,' he continues in English, 'explain more fully. What seems to be the problem?'

Mother tells Dr Kurtz that I am uncontrollable, that I am insolent, that I never do what I am told, that I am a liar and that I am destructive: I have cut up all the clothes in her wardrobe and stained them with ink. (Not *all*, I want to say. But I do not interrupt.) She goes on to explain that she finds me particularly puzzling, since her elder daughter, Charlotte, is a model of good behaviour.

'This one's a little devil!'

'You may well be on the right track, Lisa,' the doctor tells my mother quietly. 'Antonia may well be possessed. If that is the case, she will have to be exorcised.'

Kurtz takes Mother's arm and leads her to the door. Albrecht, as I am to call the little doctor, tells me to go to the corner of the room where there are toys and books, and choose what I want to play with. I go to the corner but I do not touch the toys or open a book. I turn round facing into the room and I stare at Albrecht. I am reminded of the rat from my book about the unwelcome pests Farmer Jones has to cope with on his farm. But this rat, Albrecht-rat, has spectacles that sit on the end of his long nose, and much less hair on his head than other rats.

'Tell me, Antonia, why did you cut up your mother's clothes?' His voice is quite smooth and kind, but then I remember that rats are not dangerous *all* the time.

'I didn't,' I tell him frankly.

'And why d'you lie? Don't you know that grown-ups can see right through children. We can always tell when you are lying.'

'Well, I'm not. I always tell the truth. No one believes me,' I add, 'except Walter. Walter always believes me.'

'And who is Walter?'

'He's my friend.'

'*Ach so!* And aren't your mother and father your friends? Don't you love them?'

These are difficult questions and I take my time. 'Well,' I start, hesitatingly, 'Mother and Father aren't my friends like Walter.'

'*Ach!* So you don't love them? They are not your friends and you

48

would do anything to hurt them, wouldn't you? That's a terrible thing for a little girl with such wonderful parents to do.'

'I think I do love them,' I say, but uncertainly, 'but I know they don't love me. They have some friends and they love Charlotte, my sister. I can tell because my friend Helen's mother calls her "darling" and kisses her often and gives her presents and says she's pretty and good, and my mother never does . . .'

'But you are *not* good, are you?' I cannot answer that question. I think I'm quite good but they say I'm very bad. 'I think the best thing would be if you came to talk to me tomorrow, when you've decided to tell me the truth, then we can try and discover *why* you do wicked things.'

'I don't do wicked things! I am good. I don't want to come here ever again!' I am crying and I am shouting. I run to the door but the handle is stiff and I cannot turn it and get out.

'Why do I have to go to Albrecht?'
'Because I say so!'

It is always Mother who takes me to Albrecht-rat. We go after school. Mother fetches me in the hire car, and when we get to Harley Street she goes into the rat's room before I go in alone. The rat asks me what I dream about, and whether I have seen Father without any clothes on, and whom I like and whom I don't. I think it best not to tell him anything much because like Mother and Father he always says I'm lying, and I don't like being told that because I never am. He wants to know whether Charlotte and I play together. I try to explain to him that she is five years older than I am and has her own friends, and she eats in the dining-room with Mother and Father and mostly I eat with Nanny in the nursery.

'You hardly ever see your sister?'

The rat has a way of repeating what I say and making it into a question. I hate this. I stop talking to him altogether and go into the corner and look at the books. He has some rather nice ones. And he has a toy made of wood which I like. I hammer the pegs into the holes with a mallet. I like banging at that.

One day the rat says to me: 'Antonia, there's nothing to be

ashamed of. Sometimes little children do wicked things and then, when they discover that the world doesn't come to an end – if, for example, they cut up their mother's clothes – they don't bother to do such a wicked thing again.'

'Does that mean you think I'm good, now?'

'*Ach!* So you did do that wicked thing, after all. You did cut up your mother's most cherished possessions!'

Serves me right for talking to him, I think. I shan't, not ever again.

Mother tells Father that Albrecht Kurtz says there is no point in seeing me any longer, since I refuse to talk to him. He has made arrangements for me to be seen by a play therapist three times a week.

'What's a play therapist, Mother?'

I like Barbara very much. She has a lovely little flat under the pavement so that, when I am in her room, I can see people's legs passing the window. We bake fairy cakes and make fudge, and she shows me her collection of postcards with pictures of the country-side. I discover a passion for haystacks, lakes, and mountains with snow, and when I am looking at the cards I am aware of happy feelings. I explain to Barbara that I didn't do the wicked thing they say I did. She believes me.

'I do love Mother and Father, really,' I tell her, but I feel she will understand when I tell her that it is very hard to love people who don't love you – and quite hard not to.

Barbara understands. She says I might be happier away at school, in the country. She says it's obvious I like country things – and animals and flowers – and the war is coming and I'd be safer out of London. She says she's sure that, in their hearts, Mother and Father love me very much. But when I ask her why they seem not to at all, and why it is they don't believe anything I say, she says she doesn't know.

That worries me.

'Will you come and take me out when I'm at boarding-school, Father?'

I want the girls at school to see Father in his uniform. I am

proud that Father serves his country. It's bad enough having a
foreign mother. . . .

'Don't be so selfish, Antonia. There's a war on and you're going
to have to make sacrifices too. Your father's got more important
things to do than traipse over the country to take you out to
luncheon.'

No sacrifice is too great for others to make.

'When you're on leave, please Father,' I beg.

'No, dear, it's as your mother says.'

'I notice that you still get yourself up in the most unsuitable
clothes.' Mother dragged herself on to her side. She wanted an
uninterrupted view of what she knew would be good for a critical
offensive. 'And I can't honestly say I much care for your hair-style.'

I look closely at Mother. Her eyes are hollows of dark madness.

I am fourteen. I have come to spend two weeks of my eight
weeks' holiday in Stroud with Mother and Uncle Harold. It is hot
this year. Mother insists that I accompany her to Cheltenham to
shop and while she has her hair done. One day, when she is sitting
under the dryer, having her nails manicured, I go into a bookshop.
Because it is short, I take up 'Burnt Norton' and read it right
through, standing up. It is a revelation. It has been printed on
lovely thick paper, like drawing paper, and put between greeny-
blue soft covers. It is just seven pages long. It is by someone called
T.S. Eliot. The man in the bookshop says Mr Eliot is an American
living in England. I am surprised that an American who is not in
the forces is living in England. But what interests me particularly is
that Mr Eliot suggests that the future may be contained in the
past. This is an interesting thought but one which makes me
anxious. I myself have been aware of 'unheard music hidden in the
shrubbery' since I was quite small, and Walter told me ages ago
something to the effect that 'human kind cannot bear very much
reality'. I think it was in connection with Mother. There's something about this poem: it's like an old friend. I recognize it. I love
it, too, everything about it – the title 'Burnt Norton', text, paper
and the way it's printed. I buy it and hug it to myself. I shall carry it
everywhere with me, like a talisman.

'You've become thoroughly pretentious, Antonia. Is it school that's done it to you, or have you become pretentious all by yourself? You don't impress me with your Mr Eliot. I can't imagine you understand a word of it.'

I am puzzled by Mother's snappy response to my new treasure. In order not to annoy her, I memorize the poem and put the little pamphlet at the bottom of my suitcase.

'I suppose you'll be wanting to impress your fine friends, *nicht wahr?*'

I am fifteen. All the girls of my age at school are wearing stockings. I have none. Matron writes to Mother requesting that I be sent three pairs. A letter arrives from Mother which Matron hands me to read:

> Dear Matron,
>   I received your request for stockings for Antonia. I am sure you act out of the best of intentions but I still cannot imagine what prompted you to suggest such a thing. I provide Antonia with socks because I regard them as suitable for a child of her age. Because other parents provide their daughters with stockings in no way alters my view that at fifteen socks are more fitting. Antonia may speak out as if she were a young woman but she is actually fifteen, not old enough for adult accessories.
>
>   Yours sincerely,
>   Lisa Sinclair
>
> PS. I shall not be attending prize-giving. Please inform Miss Langdale that the journey from Stroud is too long and too complicated for me – and by no stretch of the imagination could be regarded as 'necessary'.

The stain of self-interest spread to every decision my vain, peevish mother came to. I learnt later that Miss Langdale, the headmistress, regarded Mother's letter as being remarkable even by the mindless norms of other of her utterances.

I am seventeen. Mother is entertaining couples from my late father's regiment and Walter is to take his place at the end of the table, with Mother at the head. I am crossing the hall, entering the kitchen corridor behind the green-baize door at about six-thirty. Walter catches sight of me and asks me why, at this late hour, I am not changing for dinner.

'Because I'm not dining with you!' I explain that Mother has said I have nothing to say that could be remotely interesting to her guests and that my table manners are offensive.

I am not fooled by Mother. She is aware that the most dangerous times for conflict are meal-times. She does not dare risk being put on the spot. Perhaps Walter also knows this. At any rate his patience with Mother is wearing thin.

Some weeks previous to this occasion Walter is witness to an exchange between Mother and me on the topic of my clothes. He takes exception to Mother's bitter sarcasm and says as much.

'Well,' she finishes, 'don't imagine I'm allowing you to leave my house looking like that!' She is shuddering at my 'new look' dress and ankle-strap shoes. 'I suppose that look is something your upstart friends approve of.'

Mother is pitiless towards those rising towards her affluence, particularly by the sweat of their brows.

'Like what? Go on, Mother! Say it – tart!'

'How dare you speak to me like that!' She throws Walter a beseeching glance, but, deriving no support from him, thrashes around for some verbal abuse with which to sting me. 'I'll tell you this much, if ever some man is fool enough to ask you to marry him, I'll not provide a white wedding.'

'An off-white one will do nicely, Mother.'

'The trouble with you was you never learnt to do the right thing.'

I smiled when I heard those two words uttered, one after the other: 'right thing'. It was as if I had, unsuspecting, come upon some precious little memento of childhood in a junk-shop. I had forgotten the expression that encapsulated my mother's entire philosophy, the portmanteau words in which were stored all the expectations she had for herself – and for everyone else. Everyone else, of course, failed to fulfil her ideal, but Mother and Charlotte accomplished what was implied, in minute detail.

'Or have you learnt by now? Am I doing you an injustice?'

'No, Mother, I don't believe you are doing me an injustice. I don't imagine you would think I had learnt anything.'

'But, surely, a professional woman. . . .'

I closed my ears and while she spoke I thought about the things that had touched her most deeply, which she had regarded, for example, as obscene. They had had to do with her presence not being deferred to, her wishes not being met. If a servant was, as she saw it, discourteous, a child dreamy or a dog on heat, Mother was personally affronted. She felt herself to be at the very centre of the world, someone in whom was vested an undisputed right that must be acknowledged. This right, which expressed itself in an unerring capacity for doing the 'right thing', had nothing to do with social justice, nothing of fraternity in it. It was a matter of etiquette, not manners.

Mother had taken it for granted that because her parents met the expectations she had of them, they loved her. Thus she responded in kind. She had made 'a good marriage', one that would prolong the habit of material advantage she had acquired in her parents' house. For her, love was a matter of obligation: the father showed his by providing well, materially, for his family, the mother showed hers by doing the 'right thing'. The children's role was obedience. And Mother never tired of quoting Scripture to validate her point of view. She found what seemed like an endless source of material in Proverbs to which to defer, quoting them either in English or German. From earliest childhood I was made as mistrustful of God as I was of my parents. I was resentful of having to take holy as well as secular orders and admonishments. Mother told me that in days gone by, had I shown disrespect for her, I might have been thrown from the cliffs into the sea, had molten lead poured down my throat or even had my head cut off. 'Yes, child, in those days such were the punishments for children who rebelled against their parents.'

I wondered whether Mother really believed that she had loved Walter. I knew it was important for her to cling to the belief that he had loved her. The only occasion on which I could remember Mother uttering the word 'love' was to disdain my avowed feelings for the puppy, Patch. Similarly with Father. I saw no evidence of passion; I saw no evidence of caring. Mother had a permanent notice *Do not disturb* hung on her mind and her heart. I don't believe she would have entertained love. Her favourite expression was 'I could not countenance such a thing.' And I imagined her applying this liberally to the imaginative sides of life, whether sexual, emotional or intellectual.

'I fancy a Dover sole. Charlotte's been feeding me slops! If I'm dying – and I suppose I must be or I wouldn't be attracting all this attention, including your visit – I should at least be given what I want to eat. So tell Charlotte I want a grilled Dover sole and, after it, summer pudding.'

Following this exertion, Mother dropped off her elbow and lay on her side. She started to mumble incoherently, and then unexpectedly asked me whether I remembered the little sweets she used to have put in silver dishes shaped like baskets on the dining-table, to take with coffee: 'Lessiters did them. Bring me some tomorrow.' And she drifted off for a while before suddenly asking me: 'What did you bring me, Antonia?'

'A *Liebchen* rose, Mother. I knew that that would bring you all the rest.' She struggled to sit up. She rested herself unsteadily, her bony elbows jammed into her pillows. Even then, so close to death, her jaw trembled in anger.

'I hate you, Antonia! I wish I'd never had you!'

'I'm sure you don't really mean that, Mother,' I hear myself say. Why? So as not to have to answer her in kind?

'Oh yes I do! And you're not going to inherit my sables or anything else of mine. I'd rather the money went to a cats' home.'

Home! That four-letter word . . .

'I hate you! I hate you! And your father hated you, too. He didn't at first . . . but it didn't take long. . . . Remember how he used to beat you? There! That shows if ever anything does! And you monopolized Walter. . . .'

At that she fell back, exhausted.

It was then that I fully understood something I had long suspected. As a baby, I was ignored before being repudiated. A psychiatrist told me that I had narrowly avoided becoming autistic. It was only my 'solid core' that saved me, he said. Mother made no bond with me. Father may have tried to forge one of his own. But all that resulted was that Mother saw me as a threat, a rival for Father's love. For him to reassure her, they came together in an attempt systematically to demolish me by derision.

Listening to her incontinent loathing, as Mother rendered what had been and what might have been present, the past became yet more desolate for me. I was reminded of other travellers in the wilderness who, to survive, have to eat camels' sick. I needed the silence that followed her outburst to allow the full implication of her words to sink in. But I had no idea how it would affect me. There it all lay, my lonely, desolate and endangered childhood, dredged up in the present. Worse, the feeling of indifference which accompanied me to the house, earlier that afternoon, had been swept out on the last tide.

Charlotte

It was always at somebody else's expense that she
displayed her spiritual delicacy and the rigours of her
conscience.

François Mauriac

'DO LET ME PERSUADE YOU TO STAY AND HAVE A BITE TO EAT
with me. It's been so long. We've so much to catch up on. Cook is
preparing lobster thermidor' (and nice cod steaks for the kitchen, I
wondered?) 'and macerated peaches. I want to hear all about your
life and your work. Wicked little Antonia – a professor, no less.
Unmöglich! But life is full of surprises, I always say.'

'I'm not a professor, Charlotte.'

Charlotte ignored my correction and ushered me back into the
drawing-room, rather as if she were trying to pen a recalcitrant
goose. Breathlessly, without pausing to give me time to answer
her questions by staggering them, she asked whether I had kept in
touch with Helen, whether I would like to take away some of my
childhood books and toys that were still upstairs in the nursery, and
why I had chosen to wear trousers that day. 'You know Mother
can't bear to see women in trousers except on the beach. You
might have shown a little respect.'

Charlotte had never forgone an opportunity to criticize. She had
been so inclined as a child, in imitation, perhaps, of Mother.

'What's wrong with the way I'm dressed? Jeans and T-shirts are
virtually uniform these days.'

'Not in our circle, they're not.' Charlotte emphasized her observation by sniffing a non-existent dewdrop from the end of her nose.

'Look,' I tried, 'in your circle . . . a few hundred people. . . .'

But she would have none of it. 'Well, you tell me how in the
wider world things are conducted.' Charlotte had arranged her
whole body for this expression of sarcasm. I had forgotten the
Sinclair body language until that moment, yet it had been an

eloquent feature of my early life. 'How do you deport yourself? How do *you* smooth your passage through life?'

'With difficulty. I struggle . . .'

'Struggle? How do you mean, struggle? Professors earn rather handsomely, don't they?'

Who was it, I tried to remember, who complained that family life was an encroachment on private life?

Were there any complexities in Charlotte's thought? Was 'getting through life' for her merely a question of having the wherewithal to meet the bills, and enough acquaintances listed in Debrett to fill the drawing-room once or twice a year? Oh, the apathy of the secure, the insolence of wealth! It had been a struggle, but not in Charlotte's terms and I wouldn't, couldn't discuss my terms with my sister. I saw that she was feeling embarrassed and lost for words. She fiddled anxiously with her bracelet and fingered the beads under her collar. And now she wet her lips and tried the muscles of her neck.

'You always were one for complications.'

I registered in her words a sort of disgust as much as unease. (Complications of any but a physical kind were anathema in my parents' house.) She had been sitting on one of the two sofas that were placed at right angles to the fireplace. I was seated facing her. Her seated position had until then provided her with all the scope she needed for her inquiries, but for her next assault she must have felt it necessary to put more space between us, for she rose and walked to the window, turning her back on me.

'You were always one for complications,' she repeated, sighing. 'Why have you never been able to be like everyone else?'

It was a question I had often asked myself. After all, most people do what is easiest. Mother, Father and Charlotte had had it made. Why couldn't I have been like them? Of course when they said 'everyone else' they meant everyone like them, everyone from their class, and the one to which they aspired. I had never felt part of their milieu. When I was very young, I would sit quietly in a corner of the nursery watching Charlotte. She was invariably spotlessly clean, neat and composed. She had had the reputation since the age of two of being able, and willing, to eat a boiled egg neatly. This accomplishment preceded her socially and was a matter of great pride to Nanny, whose reputation among the other nannies was enhanced by Charlotte's daintinesses. I was not the subject of anybody's pride. I was rather clumsy; my dress often dirty from tree-climbing and visits to the kitchen, not to mention my incarcerations in the broom cupboard. My hair got into knots, while Charlotte's never did. My toy cupboard was in a mess and my bicycle leaked oil.

'It was most awkward socially, you know, your being so different. You used to bring comics into the house.' (Good taste meant everything to Charlotte. That was one of the reasons she was so mystified by art.) 'You have no idea how much you upset Mother with your vulgarity.'

And no doubt threatened Father. He must have been infuriated if he noticed how comics subvert authority.

Charlotte projected a quality difficult to define but easy to recognize from her tone of voice, attention to the minutiae of life and, particularly, in her relationship to possessions and money. She manifested a finiteness from which imagination was precluded. According to her, everything that related to my upbringing had not only been for the best but lacked any alternative. She was equally sure about other matters: Turks were cruel, Arabs corrupt, Americans vulgar, the working class lazy. . . . Hovering above all her utterances I sensed the angel of death.

It was the intervention of Madge, announcing that dinner was served, which rescued me. Charlotte led the way, thrusting into the dining-room like the figurehead on an ocean tub and taking her place at the head of the table. My place had been laid at her left. As my sister lowered herself into Father's seat, it crossed my mind that anyone in her circle would describe her as 'mature'. But Charlotte could never, in any real sense, mature: she was closed to experience, shut in, deaf to the entreaties of a world unrecognizable for not conforming to the Sinclair template.

It was twenty years since last I had sat at this table and shared a meal with a member of my family. Nothing of the earlier experience had been lost to time, as I imagined it would be. It all lay just below the surface of my immediate thoughts, to be awakened by the way in which Charlotte would press her foot on the bell to summon the parlourmaid, by the manner in which the silver candlesticks seemed to question the cleanliness of the dowdy drapes, and by the feel of the stiff white damask napkin I would press to my lips. Cold struck me within. I must have started, for Charlotte asked me whether I was feeling unwell. Her tone of voice expressed interest but not concern.

'It's nothing,' I reassured her. But I had forgotten: she would not want that reassurance. Physical health was Charlotte's and Mother's preferred topic. She leant towards me, hoping to savour at length the subject of my not altogether entirely reliable physical health.

To change the subject, I remarked enthusiastically of the lobster that it was delicious.

'Yes, Dawkins is an excellent cook.'

'Does she split open the poor creature alive?'

'I believe she does. She's a stickler for convention and uses the original Café de Paris recipe – the one Father insisted upon.'

There was something hideously apt in the disclosure that Father's preferred dish entailed a poor crustacean being split down its middle alive before its flesh was cooked.

'Do you remember, Antonia, when you stopped talking to us? I mean, when you were very small? One day you just stopped, gave up. You wouldn't speak to any of us – not family, servants or friends. You just wandered about the house with your teddy bear in your arms, whispering to him. Why? Do you remember?'

'I do. Something Mother said brought it back to me. You ask why? Well, I suppose a child who isn't listened to by adults is bound to seek out a substitute that will . . .'

'Perhaps you were schizophrenic as early as that . . .'

'Schizophrenic? I? Schizophrenic! What on earth are you talking about?'

'Albrecht Kurtz . . .'

'Oh my God, not him!'

'He told Mother that you were either possessed by the devil or schizophrenic.'

'I remember the possessed bit – but schizophrenic! Are you quite sure? And did Mother and Father believe him?'

'Yes, I think they did. I'm sure they did. It was after the episode of the cut-up clothes.'

'But I had nothing to do with that. I didn't do it. You know I didn't do it, don't you, Charlotte?'

'Well, at the time . . .'

'Oh, bugger "at the time"! I mean now, sitting here, you know I didn't do it, don't you?'

'Well . . .'

'Well what? Look, this is important to me.'

Over the years, I had submitted to a range of psychological tests and techniques, including hypnosis, to try to discover whether I had had a role in the cutting-of-the-clothes drama. Not a shred of evidence emerged to connect me with this act of vandalism. But I sought the truth with an anguish as terrible as my fear of finding it, for, oddly, I never wished to discover that Mother had been the culprit. I could not have weathered the knowledge of such loathing for me as that would imply.

It was after I had left home that Barbara told me quite a lot about Albrecht. He dabbled in the occult. It was actually known by others in the profession that this was an arm of his treatment. It was said that he had found a direct route to the favours of rich, bored, married women by implanting the suggestion that their emotionally disturbed children were possessed by the devil. It exonerated the mothers, it gave Albrecht scope to encourage them to confide in him how put upon they were, and to receive his sympathetic understanding as a prelude to his phallic leap. In those cases in which he encountered a resistance to the supernatural explanation, or to his advances, he substituted a medical for a psychotic diagnosis and referred mother and child to another physician. My own refusal to talk to him at all had been a more successful ploy, even a life-saving one, than I could possibly have imagined at the time.

Barbara told me that one or two reputable psychiatrists got wind of Albrecht's behaviour but closed ranks. Instead of exposing him, the best among them simply saw to it that patients were no longer referred to him.

'Well, who else would have done it?'

'Mother. One of the maids. You!'

'Really, Antonia! Why on earth would Mother have cut up her own lovely clothes, things she treasured? Mother is a vain woman, it has to be said, she was always most particular about her appearance . . .'

'Guilt?'

'And what would dear Mother have had to feel guilty about?' What would dear Mother have had *not* to feel guilty about?

'Actually, one hell of a lot. Try to imagine what it must be like to get satisfaction from your husband only if, on your instructions, he beats the daylights out of your little girl.'

'I am not going to discuss this further with you, Antonia. I can just assure you of this: Mother didn't do it and I didn't do it. I can't answer for the servants, of course.'

I felt terrible, worse in Charlotte's than in Mother's company. I wondered why. Perhaps the love that the child feels atavistically for the mother – however cruel she is – somehow survives in embryonic form and colours even the most unsatisfactory re-union. I was not conscious of ever having hated Charlotte. Had I rather despised her? Certainly I felt contempt for her now. She was speaking to me as if addressing a child, *de haut en bas*, as if I had no rights, as if I could not discriminate between what was true and what was false.

'Perhaps you have things to reproach yourself for,' I said mildly. 'Can you seriously pretend that you were quite oblivious of the abuse I was subjected to?'

Charlotte did not reply and so I continued: 'You're like the Germans, Charlotte, the ones who didn't know what was going on in the camps.'

'You were an insolent, destructive child and you had to be disciplined. Mother and Father were always good to me because I did as I was told.'

Charlotte sought the bell under the table with her foot. This treading on the servants to attract their attention was an image of my childhood that so impressed me at the time that ever after it had led me to an obsessive avoidance both of the joins in paving-stones and any insect making its way across my path. Charlotte was expanding in my mind like some inflatable doll-woman. I blinked and tried to erase that image.

'You never did as you were told. You were a little devil.'

'Tell me,' I suggested enthusiastically. 'You were close to Father. Didn't he loathe psychiatrists? Didn't he mistrust the supernatural? How come he accepted Kurtz's diagnosis – that I was either possessed or mentally deranged?'

'Father liked to believe what Mother told him,' Charlotte in-nocently allowed. 'He was a strange man,' she added thoughtfully. 'He could lead a battalion in battle but on the home front he liked to be commanded by his wife.'

Ah, the English disease. . . . Wasn't unquestioning obedience to authority one of the most disgusting and consistent of human qualities? I was surprised by Charlotte's clarity at first and then it bore in on me that she was unaware of the implications of what she said. When she added that Father was always delighted to be able to endorse Mother's opinion when the subject under discussion did not much matter to him, I registered her dig, but because she went on to say that Father was always very anxious to find ways of pleasing Mother, I let it pass and concentrated on that.

'Pity he couldn't have done so in bed!'

'That's preposterous! And *pas devant la domestique.*'

Funny how children cannot or will not accept that their parents have sex and, possibly, sexual problems. Madge had answered Charlotte's ring and was clearing the plates. Charlotte was mopping her brow on a piece of gossamer and lace, the labour, no doubt, of a virgin nun. My sister must have found it easy to switch her thoughts from those I had implanted in her, for the next thing she said was how devastated she had been when she got the letter confirming that Father was dead rather than 'missing'.

'I kept the image of him standing on the quay, waving, as my ship slipped out of Southampton docks, bound for America. I clung to this. When I heard he was dead, I never wanted to see England again.'

I was surprised. It was hard for me, with my experience of Father, to appreciate that his death was for Charlotte an absolute affliction. 'Mother didn't write to me much. I felt she had Harold and that was all she needed. I think it was the house I clung to. And then, when I did get back, I found Walter was still around . . .'

'Mother says you won't so much as let her mention his name! Why's that?'

'Don't be disingenuous. You know perfectly well why,' she condescended.

'I'm afraid I don't.'

'Walter was a most disruptive influence in the house. *And* he lived off us!' Charlotte paused. I imagine she wanted to see if this revelation shocked me. 'But he was smart. Instead of his feeling small, living off dear Mother and poor Father, he succeeded in making Father feel small. And just think how Father must have felt with Walter continuously waiting in the wings when he had to be away so much – waiting to take over his role.'

'And to take my side.'

'That too.'

'But since you managed so successfully to re-establish your relationship with Mother and have been her sole companion over all these years, why can't you go along with her on the subject of

Walter? You specifically warned *me* against jibbing at her illusions.'

'I'm not having Mother discuss her lover under Father's roof. I've never encouraged her in this and I'm not permitting it now.'

I had never heard it seriously suggested that Mother and Walter were lovers. Mother hinted at it, but that was her style – to titillate. I knew for a fact that it had never been the case. Why, I wondered, did Charlotte believe it had been? Did she want to believe it? Did she need to believe it? Did she feel that I might reveal something of my own relationship with Walter if she aroused me in some way?

'You always imagined that Walter was on your side and just for your sake,' she went on, as if to confirm my suspicions, 'but it was on Mother that he depended.' She stopped bobbing her head up and down and settled back in her chair like a jelly comfortable in its mould. 'He was forever dancing attendance on you, but it was a front. By doing what Mother didn't like, it made it seem that they were less intimate than they were.'

Oh, so that was it, was it?

'And when were Mother and Walter lovers?'

'On and off up to the time Mother heard that Father had been killed.'

How would Charlotte have known this even if it had been the case? On what did she base her assumptions?

'That was a funny time to choose to stop,' I suggested, but my sister turned a deaf ear. With unconcealed disapproval she brushed her skirt free of invisible specks.

I myself had never found an entirely satisfactory – a cast-iron – explanation for Mother's apparent tolerance of Walter's affection for me. Was it that she herself was so reliant on Walter, she did not dare to cross him? Or was it that she was positively reliant on his affection for me, which stopped her from having to occupy herself with me? Looking back over her behaviour, I can see she depended on any number of people to do for her what she neither wished to do nor was able to do. She never wholly committed herself to Walter and yet never let go of him. What was their relationship all about from her point of view? In many ways, Mother had despised Walter for making nothing (in her estimation) of himself. In Germany he had had the status of a rich playboy. In England he was, eventually, a penniless refugee with exquisite manners, seemingly available at her command. And then, when Father was no longer on the scene, this man Mother had been using as a bit-player in the drama that was her life became superannuated: he could no longer threaten the husband who had been such a personal disappointment to her. Nor was Walter much use as an escort; he was a non-commissioned officer in the Pioneer Corps. She could hardly be seen with him in uniform! Far better that he should occupy himself with the daughter she disliked and for whom (in the opinion of the law) she had become wholly responsible. Such was the legacy from her cold-fish husband and she cannot have been too pleased with it. Meanwhile, she and Harold – not the marrying kind, but one for whom the making of money came as easily as falling off a log, and for whom wartime was an auspicious time – could re-create something of Baden-Baden in Stroud.

First, they located a reliable source of food. Secondly, a poor German refugee whose passion was cookery. Their cup overflowed. Stroud was an ugly little town, but at least while Harold located and dispensed shortages – at a price – Mother could occupy herself with the ordering and disposing of excellent meals. There was something obsessional about Mother's relation to eating. It was as if her desire to have control manifested itself in her consumption.

I do not think it had occurred to me until then that Charlotte might have been jealous of me when I was little for the favour I found with Walter. On reflection, however, I could imagine the effect Walter's behaviour must have had on an adolescent girl. Charlotte was twelve when I was seven. When Walter was taking me to the ballet and the zoo, and treating me with loving acceptance, Father was frequently away from home, leaving Charlotte deprived of a male presence to confirm her. Walter must have seemed a glamorous alternative to Father. I did not notice this except in retrospect. It was not what impressed me about Walter: I loved him for loving me. But the fact that this romantically good-looking, single, available male devoted himself to me, a mere child, and ignored her, a budding young woman, must have hurt her self-esteem.

'Were you by any chance jealous of me?' I asked as kindly and calmly as I could.

'Me? Jealous of you? Come come, don't be ridiculous! What was there for me to be jealous of? *I* was the favourite child. I could do whatever I wanted – and get away with it. I could do no wrong.'

'And did you get away with things?'

'Indeed I did,' she said quickly, adding that she could not quite remember what after all these years. 'Anything I wanted to get away with, I would have succeeded in.' Charlotte smiled absently as if only partly engaged in our conversation.

It was quite obvious to me why Charlotte had never married, never had any close relationship with a member of the opposite sex. Nor had she any close women friends either. Not close, not chummy. Only rather formal acquaintances. Her emotional life had been as blighted as mine. I watched as she delicately spooned expensively macerated peaches into her lightly pinkened mouth, and dabbed her lips after each spoonful. She was composed of a string of meaningless gestures. Everything about her resonated with the assurance of one who belongs entirely and precisely where she is socially and emotionally – even geographically, for were Charlotte to be sitting in a meanly furnished room, I thought, stinking of cat and boiled whiting, she would not appear so grand, and she would not be able to make such imperious demands upon those less fortunate than herself. There is something repugnant about someone who so unquestioningly accepts her circumstances.

It was predictable that Charlotte should have returned from America impervious to all things American, to settle down in that very chair – Father's – and spend the rest of her life tending Mother. She was not merely Mother's shadow, she was Mother's guardian. She had taken the place of Father in Mother's life and no doubt fulfilled the role more satisfactorily than Father had. She too would choose to confuse a kiss and a caress with sexual possession, and a hard nature glossed over with sickly sentiment with a loving one.

'Did you enjoy living in America and going to school and college there? I remember you came back with some lovely clothes, and not a trace of an American accent.'

'I hated it! I hated every minute of those six long years. I was most unhappy as an exile, and I had such a poor education in comparison with yours. Americans are so lax about everything. Within five minutes of meeting they're on first-name terms with complete strangers who confide in you how much they earn. I spent the whole time being profoundly embarrassed about everything.' Ah yes, of course, the Sinclairs were ever and strenuously attentive to matters of form. 'I was so relieved to get back and find that Mother had managed to maintain pre-war standards.'

Charlotte twitched her head from time to time while she

delivered this intimacy.

'I was sent away, too,' I reminded her.

'Yes. But not out of the country. And you had Walter. Mother told me how he was forever rushing up to Northumberland to take you out. I had no one in America – no one of my own.'

It was true. I had had Walter. 'Is he one of your uncles?' the girls asked me. They made no secret of the fact that he reminded them of some film star or other. 'Sort of,' I allowed, wondering a little myself and knowing not to say he was a friend of Mother's. 'He was a friend of my father,' I told them, and because they knew that Father had been killed in action, they backed off. I wondered why Miss Langdale had been so tolerant of Walter. His letters to me were not opened before I got to them, his supplies went uncriticized and he suffered no interrogation when he came to take me out. I can only imagine that it was because the headmistress herself found Walter more attractive to deal with than Mother.

I remembered how there had been no question of Mother's feeding me by parcel post like the mothers of other girls. I was hungry throughout the duration; I was stuck with a jar of Marmite and a pot of peanut butter the whole term. When I wrote to Mother and asked for other items, complaining of the rubbery brown mince, the watery vegetables and the thick white suet puddings that alternated with the milk and rice under its wet-cardboard skin, I was told there was a war on.

I feared I should always remain a child with nowhere to run to. I should never graduate from my Chilprufe Liberty bodice and socks, and I would forever have Radio Malt and cod-liver oil forced down me before breakfast.

'Mother and I like to be reasonable. We can't bear people who act on impulse!'

Charlotte's words jolted me back into the present and reminded me of Walter quoting Goethe: '. . . to be uncertain is to be uncomfortable, but to be certain is ridiculous'.

'You like to be certain of things.'

'Precisely. Just so!'

I detected a note of triumph in my sister's voice.

When Charlotte returned to England, we were an all-female household. Walter's room, where before the war he would stay on the evenings he escorted Mother to the opera, after which he returned to the house for a late supper, or when there was a party at the house, or when Mother and Father were away and Walter was entertaining me, had been stripped of the Biedermeier bed and chest of drawers, and equipped as a sewing-room. A seamstress was engaged to come twice weekly to do such jobs as in the past had fallen to Nanny. I was secretly pleased that Father was no longer part of the household. I wrestled with myself, trying to absolve myself from uneasy feelings of guilt for being relieved that he was dead. I told myself that I should be just as satisfied if he were alive – in Australia. I was no longer in perpetual fear. Even on seemingly normal outings I dreaded being with Father in case he attacked a mannerless shop assistant or uncooperative waiter out of habit. I was not frightened of Mother as I had been of Father. If she were to lurch into an attack on me now, I should be able to defend myself. It was Father's physical strength, his lack of control over his temper – and their combined conspiracy – that had so wounded me. Without that, with just Mother's contempt to cope with, I thought I could manage. However, I did not quite succeed in doing so. My anger at the brutalities of the past at home and the way in which I had been exiled to a school that was unsuited to my intellectual needs, where I had been bored and lonely, turned in on me and I became chronically depressed.

When I was still quite young and undergoing regular punishment for things I had not done, or for misdemeanours which merited only a light rebuke, I knew that however lonely and hopeless I felt – and often hungry for being sent to bed without supper – the next day I would feel better. I seemed to be like those dolls filled with shot that cannot be toppled. But when I got to boarding-school, I found that the experience of cold, loneliness, hopelessness and hunger did not miraculously evaporate. Depression lasted longer and longer as I grew older. By the time the war was over and I was back in London, attending a first-class day-school, I was almost continually depressed.

'You were so precious to Mother and Father. They needed to be absolutely confident that you were somewhere completely safe. With hindsight, I can see it would have been far better if you had gone to Northumberland and I had been shipped out to Vermont.'

I was here under the family roof. It was for the last time. I would not want to see Charlotte again – and I would not have to see Mother again. Perhaps, for my own peace of mind, I should find out more than I knew about Charlotte. And about Father. Perhaps

I should ask Charlotte for the names and addresses of one or two of Father's old messmates.

'Would you have liked a profession?' I asked my sister. 'Do you feel you've rather wasted your life?' I could tell at once that I had not been as tactful as I might.

'Good gracious, what a suggestion! Of course not! Ever since coming back from dreadful America, I've thoroughly enjoyed myself. Mother and I have kept busy, what with one thing and another. . . .'

And time was there to be filled rather than explored. Being busy was being virtuous. Following a profession – unless in the arts and crafts – was unfeminine, Mother had told me. Knowledge was for men. Charlotte was not expected to make money.

I watched as she finished her cheese. Like an owl catching a mouse she closed her eyes when she placed the piece of cheese and biscuit in her mouth. I looked away. It irritated me to watch Charlotte refuelling. 'Where is the nurse eating?' I asked, longing to ask, too, *what* she was eating.

'In the servants' sitting-room. But she'll be popping in and out of Mother's room. I think it would have embarrassed her to eat with us. It's been most fortunate that my health has held up,' she added quickly, turning the conversation away from a possible minefield. I had forgotten that, ever since she was a child, Charlotte had shared with Mother an obsession with health – their own, of course.

'Are you happy these days, Antonia?'

'Since only the past is truly happy and mine was not, how could I be?'

'Always the clever riposte!'

The corners of Charlotte's mouth demanded the immediate attentions of her napkin, and while she dabbed I considered what in Charlotte's lexicon happiness implied. What sort of things made Charlotte happy? How would she express joy? Surely Charlotte would take self-satisfaction as happiness. She had neither the simplicity, the objectivity nor the self-forgetfulness required for an experience of the real thing. Mother had always affected an absence of happiness, a perpetual distress occasioned by the unfulfilled promise made at Schloss Huberman when she was twelve. A sort of in-the-circumstances-I-have-learnt-to-make-the-best-of-things-as-they-are. But this was invariably followed up by a homily on the subject of the folly of the pursuit of happiness, anyhow, with built-in confusion regarding the difference between happiness and joy. Looking back, I imagine that Charlotte, in an effort to emulate Mother, would have affected the same outward mien of someone who justifies her own inability to appreciate life at an immediate, sensuous level with the oft-quoted remark of Mother's that we are not put on earth to be happy. In the event, I savoured the memory of my years of ecstasy and felt the tears pricking the back of my eyes.

'Yes,' I murmured, 'I've found a sort of contentment. And you?'

'Oh, I'm perfectly happy. I have everything I want.'

She was clearly on the defensive, and yet her display of certainty sickened me. I did not feel 'poor Charlotte' as I felt I should. I felt 'Serves you damn well right!' Hers was a life of duty from which she gained the appearance of respect that quickly translated itself into self-esteem.

'I shall miss Mother, of course. But she's had a good life and she's been very ill, and although I shall be bound to feel a great chasm in my life, I can't expect Mother to live for ever now, just because I enjoy looking after her, can I?'

Oh the sweet reasonableness! The rumpety-tum of that rehearsal, intended to convey my sister's unselfish devotion, but which did no more than strike me the way a popular ditty strikes: indelible but vacuous. It proved that Charlotte knew nothing of passionate love, the love that expects and demands the beloved to live for ever, against all odds, never to die, never to abandon you.

'It makes me happy to know I'm doing the right thing.'

Aristotelian, no less!

'We'll take coffee in the drawing-room.' Charlotte pushed her foot down on the bell and her chair back. She screwed her napkin in her fist and let it fall on the table.

Coffee! After-dinner coffee! The harlequin cups. . . . In a fraction of a second, one of Mother's past rituals returned. Mother had collected antique coffee-cups on her travels and others from antique shops in London. Some she had brought from Germany in her trousseau. She was obsessively attached to these cups and would wash them up herself after a dinner party, so determined she was that not a single one should get broken. When pouring coffee she considered the dress of the woman, the tie of the man, and she matched the cup she passed accordingly. 'The little Limoges, Grace, goes most beautifully with your complexion,' she would say when Grace's dress seemed to demand the least attention possible. 'Harry, the Chelsea reminds me so of those lovely cherries from your tree', when, in fact, it was reminding her to the exclusion of all else of the wart on his nose. 'Lisa has such taste! Such originality!' And Mother would preen herself. She was remembered for this ritual. She did not have to devise an original thought or be mindful of the special interests of her guests, she simply passed the coffee-cups.

The tension that had been mounting eased a little as Charlotte and I made our way from the dining-room into the drawing-room, but I noticed that whereas Charlotte over the years had adopted Mother's mantle, my reaction to the past remained resolutely my own. And so my reaction to Charlotte was not the same as my reaction to Mother. This pained me. I had to face the uncomfortable memory that I yearned for Mother's love when I was small, but that I had not cared about my sister. Mother's acts had run through me, pierced my heart and lacerated my feelings, whereas Charlotte's lay on my consciousness like a fine film of dust. Charlotte was no danger to me. I would get through the evening.

Charlotte passed me the Newport cup. She held the silver cream jug over the cup and raised her eyebrows. I shook my head.

'Do you remember Marguerite Rayne?' she asked.

I nodded.

'When this is all over,' she lowered her voice and narrowed her eyes and I was to understand that she referred to Mother's life, 'Marguerite and I are going away for a little rest. I really need it. These past months have been most trying.' She rolled the humbug around in her mouth.

'What a good idea!' I said encouragingly.

'She has to live rather modestly and she doesn't get the opportunity for much travel, so she's quite pleased to join forces with me.'

'And where do you plan to go?'

'Lake Garda.'

I was tickled that Charlotte had planned this holiday, after carefully calculating, no doubt, that by the dates for which she had made her reservations Mother would have given up the ghost. Like that of many people, the tone in which she made her calculations was pious: 'I know Mother would want this.'

'Tell me about Father, Charlotte. And about Granny Sinclair. I remember so little about her. And did Mother ever speak about her parents? Did she mourn them?'

Charlotte put down the little Meissen cup, rose and walked over to the chimney-piece and the bell-pull. 'Some other time,' she murmured, looking tense. She waited, leaning against the chimney-piece, until Madge entered. Then she said: 'Ask the nurse to come and see me.'

At the very moment I expressed an interest in filling some gaps in my knowledge about the family, Charlotte switched off.

It took a while for the nurse to appear. I wondered what was detaining her. Was some important stage in the process of dying taking place? I knew nothing of lingering death. I felt unease. When the nurse finally presented herself – cool, crisp and unhurried – such thoughts were banished perfunctorily. Mother, she informed us, was sleeping peacefully but 'it won't be long now'. She would call Charlotte when Mother showed signs of regaining consciousness or of slipping away. Either might occur quite shortly.

'Wouldn't you rather sit with Mother?' I asked Charlotte.

'No,' she answered, entertaining thoughts of her own.

I wondered whether they were of matters unknown to me, but I dismissed the idea. Charlotte was not capable of any but domestic thoughts. Why did she not want to sit with Mother? Would the emotional strain be too much for her? If she loved Mother so much. . . . But of course she had already done her fair share. . . . I was, however, surprised that, with the time before us just waiting, she did not want to talk about the family, independently of their attitude and behaviour towards me. It was as if she thought it no business of mine, that I was an outsider. And yet it was she who had asked me to come along. There is nothing at the heart of an onion, I found myself thinking.

We sat in silence, listening to the tick of the clock and the beat of our hearts. I should like to have got up and left there and then. I think Charlotte's refusal to inform me, to deny me the information I needed to flesh out my own partial view, was the worst aspect of the aggression she was showing me. A sort of panic overtook me: I felt rooted to the spot. And walking across the drawing-room, opening the door on to the hall, taking down my jacket from the coat-stand and opening the front door, seemed impossible obstacles.

I was sickened by my sister. What I could make out of her made me uneasy, but there was much I could not fathom at all. She had always had a need to be right, rather than interesting. Despite her apparent stability, she seemed insecure. Long ago, she had been sent away from Mother and Father. It was for her own safety, but it had seemed to her that she had been rejected, and worse, that by her absence she had forfeited Father for all time. Did she feel guilt as well as anger? Did she feel that, had she refused to leave, shown some fibre, she might in some superhuman way have saved Father's life? In her absence Walter and Uncle Harold had usurped her place. . . . The fact that, finally, she had managed to get Mother to herself could never make up for, or explain, behaviour that went before. She must be suffering, thinking that Mother was slipping away from her. I understood something of what she might be feeling, but I had no sympathy for Charlotte. All my life I had watched as she contentedly did what was expected of her. What was expected was always eminently practical. She was totally without imagination. In some way, it was her lack of imagination that made me dislike her so much. She could never see beyond the end of her nose.

School had left me a terrible legacy. From the prison called home I was exiled to another, less materially comfortable one, called St Gudula's. Clothed as I was in navy from my flannel knickers to my serge tunic, bored from morning to night, compulsorily exercised, badly and inadequately fed, my company consisted of other girls whose parents were rich enough and indifferent enough to consign them to the care of unqualified staff. Our letters were often intercepted and our reading material censored. Our valuables were removed from us, so that without a watch I was at first disorientated and later learnt to tell the time to the minute by my interior clock. We were not asked to do this and that, but ordered, and if we did not respond positively and immediately, we were punished. Everything was done to a timetable: eating, washing, getting up and going to bed.

When the front door of St Gudula's shut behind me for the first time, I felt I had left myself behind, on the bleak Northumberland sands with the wading birds. I had been sent into exile. I looked back and noticed the door was already locked. I felt as fragile as one of the birds' eggshells. I took in a breath and my nostrils were immediately filled with the smell of plimsoles, sweat and bleach, and something I later discovered to be a thick, ochre fluid used to wash the hair of girls who had failed to wear their velour hats on the train and might be harbouring nits.

I believed that, had I come from a loving home, I should either have been removed from this institution on demand, or I should have been able to put up with the rigours of the regime, accepting that in wartime there were worse things being suffered elsewhere, and knowing that I could share the most flagrant injustices and discomforts with kind parents who would help me laugh the perfidies away. But being lonely inside and out of this prison was an intolerable burden for a nine-year-old to carry.

Yet it was no good my assuming that my own ghastly experiences had been worse than Charlotte's. Charlotte had had the whole breadth of the Atlantic between her and her only surviving parent. School for me had been mean and depressing, filled with unimaginative children willing to absorb unquestioningly the conventional untruths warmed up for them rather than cause trouble. The bad children, who questioned – of whom I was held to be the worst – were further isolated and punished and ridiculed. To cap it all, I had no parents to visit me. On the Saturdays and Sundays when the more fortunate girls were taken out to a meal, a film or a local fair, I had to wander desolate in the fields or along the sea-shore. What had I done, I wondered, to bring down this rejection on my head? Who knows what Charlotte went through?

I recalled my humiliation with terror. Never since childhood had I felt quite the abandon I experienced during my years in Northumberland. Had Charlotte been irrevocably stained and mutilated by her exile? Had she entertained the suspicion that Mother did not really love her? And had she stuck like glue to Mother's side ever since to make up for a deprivation she had come to know was inevitable, having discovered that Mother was not capable of love, only dependence?

When I was a child I wanted Mother not only to love me but to do so in a demonstrative way. Had she been the devil incarnate (which, subsequently, I often thought she was), yet capable of love and its expression, I would have accepted it and her unquestioningly, willingly. But added to her coldness there was her capriciousness. I never knew how she would respond to me, if it would be to insult me, hit me or lock me out.

On my walk back from day-school, both before and after the war, I used to buy flowers for Mother: snowdrops in winter, anemones in autumn, stocks in summer.

'They're pretty,' she would say languidly, continuing to polish her nails as I held out the bunch and the parlourmaid poured afternoon tea. Mother always rested (exhausted from idleness) in the afternoons, and when I returned from school I was required to go to her dressing-room, ask her politely how her health was and tell her what had happened at school that day. Not that she listened to me; I would say we did this or that, and while I was explaining, Mother was asking for a cucumber sandwich to be passed to her. I would say that I had received a red star and she would interrupt, 'Just a minute, Antonia', and call out to the maid, who was doing something in the adjoining bedroom, to put out such and such a dress and shoes for the evening and remind her to make a particular telephone call later in the day. And then she might order me to go to the nursery. 'I have things to discuss with Nanny.' I knew that 'things' were me. I knew that some reprimand was under consideration.

No beating, no cruel words, no denial of privileges equalled the desolation of my Northumberland years. Much later in life I came to acknowledge the extent to which material comfort can alleviate psychological discomfort and emotional neglect. I always knew that whatever happened I could afford a roof over my head and food. Without that assurance, I wonder what might have befallen me.

It looked as if Mother was going to die before I had had my say. But had that not always been on the cards? I felt I should go up to her room, shake her into consciousness and upbraid her for ruining my childhood and infecting my adulthood. But my feelings were so contradictory. I was dismayed by them. On the one hand I wanted to find the strength to avenge the abuse she had heaped on me. On the other hand, I wanted her to apologize so that I might find the grace to forgive her. But were I to find such grace, how would I express it? Certainly not with hugs and kisses. I couldn't abide the idea of taking Mother's hand, let alone placing my lips against her forehead. And why the charade? If I managed to forgive, it would be with my brain not my heart. The early deposits of love are irretrievable. Maybe I ought to have felt differently, but in matters of experience there are no oughts.

It would serve her right to learn about Walter and me! Unwittingly she had handed on to me a unique experience of friendship, passion – and something ineffable. I wanted to gloat. That would finish her off! But if my thoughts raced over the sticks and stones, and the more fertile planes of my existence, my body felt dead. I could not so much as raise my arm. I should certainly not be able to put one foot down in front of the other. I looked over at Charlotte. Flesh of the same flesh! How could that be?

'And what I always say is this: . . .'

I did not listen, neither did I hear. Prissy sissy, prissy sissy, I thought. She and Mother: the pair of them! They'd do a lot better to concentrate on being human rather than ladylike. . . .

I imagine that had anyone been able to read my thoughts as I considered the expensive but ugly decorative pieces in my mother's house, and regretted my lost innocence, they would have detected a range of regrets. How dearly I should have liked to be brought up among beautiful things; how dearly I should have liked to conserve my innocence! I studied Charlotte's face. All I saw was a mask. Charlotte had accumulated a range of gestures and facial expressions to convey her opinions and feelings, no doubt in an effort to spare her the inconvenience of having to exchange words with strangers and servants. However, with me, on whom she was intent on leaving an unforgettable impression, she gathered her energies and forged sentences with built-in reproach to garnish the looks she cast: the sniff prepondered. But there was, too, the rearrangement of the shoulders, along with the dramatic shaking of the table napkin, the tap-tapping of the fingers on the arm of the chair. Into my mind shot the cracking of the knuckles on a broad hand. Father's. And then I remembered how, when I was a child first exploring the world of books, Charlotte – because she had not heard of a particular author – would lower the corners of her mouth and toss her head to suggest by these gestures that the writer I mentioned did not exist.

'I want you to promise me you'll say something kind to Mother to ease her departing.'

What a nerve!

'I really think you have extraordinary cheek, Charlotte! Leave it to me to decide whether I should forgive Mother for abusing me, and ordering Father to do so. You speak as if they merely made a few mistakes in bringing me up.' And I thought how important it is to forgive mistakes and how one must be able to distinguish between a genuine error of judgement and wilful cruelty.

'You are wicked, Antonia! You were born wicked and you have grown into a wicked woman!' Her face flushed and her lips pursed. The skin on her face tightened.

'Tell me,' I asked as calmly as I was able, 'how is a tiny mite wicked? Did I gas the neighbour's dog? Did I betray Father to Mother and Mother to Father? Did I show signs of envy, pride, wrath, lust, gluttony, avarice and sloth at three years of age? I may well have indulged my sweet tooth and dragged my feet a little, but remind me by what behaviour did I exhibit signs of other deadly sins? I was neither morally depraved nor malicious – despite examples of both. And *I* never tried to emulate our parents. . . .'

And as I thought back I realized that the attacks on my so-called wickedness had probably given me some strength. In their efforts to crush me they had fortified me. But my strength must have been regarded as devilish and given them the corroboration they sought.

My outburst had the effect of making Charlotte freeze. Nevertheless, I detected the merest smirk playing round her ungenerous mouth: she knew that she had won this round. And having won a round, she was satisfied to rest in her corner. What, I wondered, would the next bout bring?

'I have made all the arrangements. The whole thing will be conducted like a military operation. Father would have wanted that. I have left nothing to chance. The undertakers have had their instructions well in advance. So has the florist. I've drafted the obituary for *The Times* and *The Telegraph*.'

Charlotte fished for a piece of paper lying under a book on the small table at her elbow and handed it over to me. It stated that Lisa Sinclair, née Bergner, was not only the widow of George Dawson Sinclair, DSO, but the 'beloved' mother of Antonia and Charlotte. This I could not, would not, tolerate. 'No, Charlotte!' I insisted. 'Yes, Antonia!' she parried. 'Oh, what the hell!' I conceded.

'I shall be selling the house. . . . It's too large for one. I shall have to dispose of a lot of the furniture and so on, I'm afraid . . .'

'Don't be! I can manage well enough with what I have.' Unlike Mother and Charlotte, who would have hired Escoffier to open a tin of sardines on Cook's night off, I could look after myself in every particular. 'I've known for years', I told my sister, 'that the price of independence is disinheritance.'

Money, together with 'personal matters' and politics, had never been subject for discussion in the family in my presence. I was, however, made aware that with money came respect; it was because the servants had none of the former that they did not receive much of the latter. This state of affairs had the effect of making me feel disturbed and frightened.

It was Uncle Harold who liked to talk about money. He told me, one holiday in Stroud, how Mother had got her sizeable fortune out of Germany 'just in time', and how she would not have been able to keep up the house in the avenue as she had in the past, or contributed so generously to charity, if all she had been left with was a brigadier's pension.

I did not want Charlotte to share the spoils with me. If she had suggested doing so, I should have known that it was not from spontaneous generosity, with which I might well have been able to cope, but from some calculation or other that I would not understand but that would trouble me endlessly.

'Mother is such a good person. Everyone says so. The ladies on our committees have looked to her as an example, as I always have.'

'You'll have to become your own mother now,' I heard myself say.

'Whatever that might mean,' Charlotte snapped back.

I could understand her irritation. This sort of remark is bad enough when directed at someone who knows the jargon of psychotherapy. It is incomprehensible to those who do not.

'It's the legacy of Mother and Father's principles that I most value,' Charlotte confided.

And while she elaborated on the theme of principles I recalled Mother's blind partiality, her unstoppable self-serving, and Father's perfidy.

'Hitler had principles,' I said tonelessly. 'What on earth's the virtue of adhering to principles that are corrupt?'

'Hitler? Corrupt? How dare you speak of Mother and Father in the same breath. Wash your mouth out, Antonia! Remember this: the King honoured Father. As for Mother, when I think of the way in which she has spent herself in the service of the less fortunate. . . . What, may I ask, have you done to compare to what Mother and Father did?' I hoped nothing. 'And what have you to grumble about? You were just as well looked after materially as I.' When did they play with me? When did they listen to me? When did they chat with me, walk with me, read to me? 'Would you rather have been born into a poor family? You may well not have got away with being difficult among the poor. Tell me, what precisely did you want from Mother?'

'"One who made no claims, But simply loved because that was her nature."'

Someone calm and kind and wise: a reassuring presence. Not someone vain, inconsistent and peevish . . . not someone who, on

Nanny's day out, obliged to 'take care' of me, has left me with the memory of being dragged along the street and only stopping to be slapped across the face, ridiculed and verbally abused. . . .

'Each of us has to play the hand we're dealt. Mother and Father did their best. They meant well.'

'They may have done their best. They certainly didn't mean well.'

'They were children of their time and their backgrounds. Mother was a foreigner in England – and a Jew. No doubt she felt insecure among the English. She needed rules to follow scrupulously. Father knew all about rules and discipline and liked to apply both. I can see how nicely they accommodated one another. I must say, I liked their way. I liked it a lot better than the *laissez-faire* of America. You might have preferred America,' she added thoughtfully. 'Do you like living alone?' she then asked vaguely.

I could not tell whether this was a challenge, for throughout the afternoon and evening I had been constantly aware that she asked only those questions for which she felt she had an answer to refute my own. Was she merely making conversation? No, of course, I loathe it, forever pretending that I am alone from choice. 'You are so efficient,' people tell me, but I am not complete, as they also insist. How is it possible to unknow the known? How could I, today, share my living-quarters with someone with whom I could share only *part* of my life? Of course I loathe being at the mercy of spare men to take me to the theatre and sit next to me at extravagantly contrived dinner parties. Spare men are not spare for nothing: they are invariably men with emotional and sexual problems, with protruding lower lips and stomachs to match.

'Yes,' I lied, 'I like living alone. I like being able to do what I want, when I want.' And by adding this rider, I satisfied myself that there was some truth in my utterance.

'I should have thought it lonely. . . .'

Was Charlotte remembering America? I had started to understand that, since the end of the war, everything she had done and become resulted from her experiences there, and her overriding desire not to find herself again without a parent. The only years in which I had not been lonely were those between nineteen and twenty-nine, when the gift of faithful friendship and passionate love had combined in a rapturous experience that nothing else could ever approach. However, this was not a conversation I wished to pursue with my sister.

'I'm going to be so lonely.'

I looked at Charlotte. I saw fear in her eyes. Real fear. Gone the fancy gestures, the facial grimaces. A sort of blank stare flooded her face. I could not tell if she was aware of the tears oozing from the corners of her eyes.

'You know a lot of people,' I tried.

'Yes, I do. You're quite right. I'm being very silly.' And truly grateful to me, she rose to tidy a perfectly neat pile of magazines on the sofa table. I saw her take a handkerchief from her pocket and dab her eyes. 'I want you to know, Antonia, I'm very pleased you came home to see Mother and me. You did the right thing. And there's no place like home, is there? I'm so glad I've been able to keep Mother at home. It would have been an unbearable offence for her to have had to die in some nursing home. She's made this house so lovely. Just look about you at all her beautiful things. What impeccable taste!'

'A gilded cage is no less a cage . . .'

'A cage! Really, how can you call your lovely home a cage? Be truthful. At heart, don't you miss all this?' And she swept her arm in the air, indicating house, garden, treasures – and comfort.

'No, it's a blessing to be free of it all.'

And I carefully refrained from exposing to Charlotte the fact that, to this day, there were certain colours and textures, certain pieces of china, glass and silver that I had only to glimpse in a shop window to feel sad, lonely and despised again; and others, together with scents and sounds, that filled me with nostalgic longing. The first could be traced to 'home'; the second to Walter. It was as if, located inside me, was a repository of films activated by a sensory mechanism. I lived permanently on the perimeter of the past. I had acquired a technique for balancing most of the time, but if caught unawares I lurched one way into feelings of irrecoverable delight, or the other, on a descent into hell.

Why had I acceded to Charlotte's request to 'come home' and see Mother before she died? It seemed at the time that I was accepting because it was easier than declining. Five hours closeted at home, and the scars of the old wounds were split open and gaping, while the acid being poured generously on to them was etching my bones. It was only when I came face to face with Mother that certain incidents of my childhood had returned and I had been obliged to relive them. The house itself – its pretentious grandeur, its *objets* that had always been more precious to my parents than animal and human life, its veneered surface maintained in an effort to gloss over the corruption at its core – reinforced Mother's words. I wondered whether to go into Father's study and complete the horror, but seeing his Sam Browne belt and cane, his revolver, might be too much. I got up and walked to the window. The sun was sinking behind the cedar, casting long shadows across the lawn. I fancied I heard an echo.

'Do you mind?' I inquired, opening one of the french windows.

'Not at all.'

Please God she will not follow me. Thirty years ago – even twenty – I had loved this garden. It had seemed not to belong to Mother and Father but to Mr Henderson who worked it, to me who played in it, and to Walter and me on walks which held the promise of better times ahead. I wandered down to the pond. The goldfish had gone, the water-lilies no longer cupped their yellow faces in white, waxy hands. The water-boatmen had ceased their skidding across the lily pads, for the pool was drained, dry and brown-edged.

> Go, go, go, said the bird: human kind
> Cannot bear very much reality. . . .
> What might have been and what has been
> Point to one end, which is always present.

I walked on, up the steps to the summer-house. The paint was blistered and flaking, the windows smeared. It was locked, and when I pressed my face against the windows, I saw that the little refuge was being used for storage. There, with Mr Henderson's lawn-mower, spade, fork, rake, scythe, dibber and twine, was neatly folded in its canvas sling my wigwam. My favourite toy! I fancied I could feel the coarse, stiff stuff and smell the scent of air trapped inside the tent on a hot summer's day. I used to erect the wigwam in the orchard and conceal myself in it, doing nothing but experience the peculiar light filtering through the orange-red painted canvas. No one was permitted entrance – or perhaps had never requested entrance. At any rate I felt safe in the wigwam and as contented as I ever managed to feel in the awesome circumstances of my childhood. I tried the summer-house door but it was locked. I would ask Charlotte for the wigwam. God knew what I would do with it. I had another much safer place of bricks and mortar in which to conceal myself these days.

I opened the gate in the picket fence and walked into the orchard. The trees were heavy with fruit, their boughs bending under the weight of the finest species. Why did no one pick it? I did not imagine that Charlotte made jams and jellies, chutneys and cordials, but what about Cook? And then I remembered that Charlotte had laid her plans: she was going to move out just as soon as Mother moved on. . . . I picked an apple and crunched the exquisite fruit as I walked back into the formal garden, stopping to stroke the beckoning stone Roman, the fawn and the lady's cornucopia, as overflowing with bounty as it had ever been, but rather weather-beaten since last I had examined its unchanging contents. I must ask Charlotte whether Mr Henderson still looked after the garden. His peacock, shaped from the box tree, had lost none of its haughtiness, and the lead cistern was planted out with the same varieties of plants as in my childhood: silver-leafed foliage, deep purple verbena, petunias. In the corner of the orchard I noticed a pile of wooden planks. Mr Henderson's tool-shed was no more. That was why he was using the summer-house.

'Would you like to go upstairs into the nursery and your old room and collect what remains of your things?'

Such as? But I could not tell Charlotte that I was frightened to go up to the second floor, to the nursery – to what purpose had it been put? – or the little room in which I had so often been confined against my will. Nor could I refuse myself the confrontation.

I should have to think more deeply about memory. It was significant, I realized for the first time, that I spent my professional life foraging in the past and yet for years had strenuously avoided foraging in my own. As I mounted the stairs I was back in the terror: every day a pogrom.

But memory is perfidious. Why, when I could so clearly relive the experience of hurt to my heart and soul, could I not re-create the bruising and lacerations of my flesh and the breaking of my bones to show the world? Why is it so contrived that the body has no memory? Someone, I had heard, was inventing a weapon that destroyed men but not buildings. How utterly appropriate! I was surprised Father had not had a hand in it.

My unlived-in room conveyed a similar desolation to that which I carried with me in one of the chambers of my mind. I cannot bring myself to describe the room – the tophet, as I came to think of it. I don't want to be reminded of Mr Bear, his yellow fur worn down in patches by numberless intimate confidences accompanied by hugs and kisses. His leather nose had survived, and his lovely deep-brown glass eyes. I put him quickly into a plastic bag (worried lest he would not be able to breathe) and gathered up three *John and Mary* books – stories of happy family life in which I used to immerse myself – and some *Milly-Molly-Mandy* ones. I had not thought of these titles since the war. And there was my inlaid walnut box in which I kept small treasures – shells, cigarette cards, badges. I must have that! But would I ever dare open it? I unlatched the cupboard door but there was only an echoing emptiness. On the bedside table sat an old-fashioned alarm clock, such as was supplied to each of the servants, and a lamp with a parchment shade on which was printed a map of Europe. I recognized neither of these objects as having been my own. The little window faced on to the orchard and I could make out the old elm fruit-picking ladder standing against the Victoria plum tree and, just behind, near the hedge of flowering currant, the place where I used to put up the wigwam. I did not linger in that bleak little room, my *oubliette*. How small everything had become!

'Do you still have Mr Henderson?'

'His son. The old man is not up to it these days.'

'Why isn't the fruit being picked?'

'It will be. I've arranged for some of the ladies on my musicians' committee to pick it for our forthcoming sale.'

'What a good idea!'

'Did you take the things you want? Anything you don't take will be sold at auction, I'm afraid.'

'Could I have the wigwam?'

'The what?'

I found myself reminding Charlotte of an occasion I had not thought about since I had left home for good.

'Do you remember when Mother and Father took us to Hamleys once in the summer holidays? I think we went by taxi and I remember how happy everyone was. Father couldn't understand why on earth I wanted to be an "injun", but he said I could have the wigwam and he even set it up for me in the garden when we got home.'

'Yes . . . and I got a fairy cycle. I was so proud of it. Afterwards we had ice-cream sundaes at the soda fountain at Selfridges. . . .

That was a lovely day.'

For a few moments Charlotte and I shared a serene recollection. A sort of agony constricted my breathing. Shouldn't the whole of childhood be composed of such memories: sunny, shared and without contention? Charlotte found the key to the summerhouse and handed it to me.

'Why did you want a wigwam?'

'I can't remember why exactly, but it became my most precious possession.'

'You used to hide in it.'

Madge was detailed to pack the books, the wigwam, the walnut box and Mr Bear in a canvas holdall. She volunteered to pick me some apples from a low-slung branch of the scarlet nonpareil and include them. Organizing these things had involved Charlotte in her familiar role, and she had clearly enjoyed the extrapersonal nature of the negotiations. She offered me a brandy and asked Madge to bring more coffee. During my absence in the garden she had been up to Mother. Mother was sleeping peacefully, and the nurse told my sister that Mother was now likely to survive into the night. Charlotte and I had more hours to get through together. Uncontentious topics of conversation were running out.

'Did you ever think of marrying?' I asked my sister.

'Of course I've had men friends,' she replied thoughtfully, sidestepping my question. 'There's never been anyone with whom I wished to share my life. . . . There's always been Mother to consider and, frankly, I've never met a man who could come up to the very high standards set by Father. I like a man of authority. I like a man who knows how to order wine, who knows how to dress,' she added wistfully.

I was astonished at how equably Charlotte spoke, as if almost to herself, and of what trivialities. I wondered whether she had given the marriage contract itself some thought and decided that, since she did not need to be 'kept', there was little point in agreeing to sexual congress and domestic chores until death-do-us-part. It would not have conferred status on her; she was better off on her own. And yet I felt that the subject was a painful one for her; the implications of what she said about Father had probably never aroused her curiosity.

Between Charlotte and all she avoided considering yawned an unplumbed chasm of emotional distance. She could not entertain the spontaneous and the unexpected. She ignored the unfathomable. Her days suited her as they were; she liked her time to extend uncommitted so she could fill it with her little range of pre-selected activities. She had taken the drudgery out of life – as she saw it. In fact she had taken the zest.

When once time had strolled for me, Walter and I would stretch it out aimlessly in idleness. We lived in a sort of dream. There were no obstacles to overcome, no differences to negotiate. The unexpected was our entertainment. Just sitting in a room together with books, without books, with a bottle of wine, without a bottle of wine – whatever the contingencies – was idyllic. There were times when money was short and times when it was flush. Neither was better than the other. As I brought into focus the image of Walter and me sitting talking over the shop in Camden Town, I suddenly imagined Mother watching us. I felt myself caught by the wrists, then by the arms, shaken, slapped, and a great blow land on my cheek. A tooth came loose in my mouth. As I spat it out, I spat a rivulet of blood.

'No you won't! You won't go to the pantomime with Walter!'

I felt along my gums with my tongue. There was no pain. My teeth were intact. But my head felt as if it were bound tightly in bandages of wire and string. I tore myself back into the present.

'Are you feeling all right?'

'Yes, why?'

'I thought you looked a little off-colour suddenly.'

I should have liked to ask Charlotte for further details but I should not have wished to elaborate myself. Instead I said: 'Do you know, I've forgotten almost everything about Father except the beatings inflicted on me. What do you remember of him?'

'He was a man who had heroes. I remember particularly how he admired the King.' Charlotte paused to reflect and savour this memory and I did not interrupt her. 'He played the piano divinely. He danced elegantly – ballroom, of course. And I could always rely on him. I knew he loved me. He didn't have to tell me so or smother me with kisses. He used to pore over my homework with me when he was at home. He used to take me up to the barracks to see the horses. He promised me a horse when the war was over. . . . On special occasions he took me to tea at Gunters. On the way there and back he pointed out landmarks to me, the Marble Arch, the Horse Guards, you know the sort of thing. He knew London like the back of his hand and he was so knowledge-able about British history. On one of our outings he bought me a coral necklace. He was very particular about how I looked, how Mother dressed me.'

Charlotte spoke dreamily with a faint smile on her face. I felt the blood flood my checks. This man my sister was bringing to life was my father too, the father who insulted me for being plain, who never gave me anything – unless you can call sound hidings 'anything'.

'He was very proud of my appearance. He used to remark of my posture that none of his men had anything to teach me about standing up straight.'

'Stand up straight, Antonia! Straight, I say! You look like some sort of baboon. I'm truly ashamed of you!'

Whatever Charlotte said, I believe that Father agreed with Freud that womanhood is a failed form of masculinity.

Had I been jealous of Charlotte? I must have craved Father's love. And how was it I hit on the idea of transferring my love for Father – and my need for its return – to Walter? Had Walter conspired in this?

Perhaps my sister and I did have something in common. Perhaps it is as damaging to the preferred child to seem to be cast off at fourteen as it is for the despised child to be abused from earliest recollection, for the power of the damage to our psyches has so much to do with the mixed signals we receive. Only rarely had I to receive medical attention for the physical abuse meted out to me. Charlotte was well cared for in America, whatever she felt about her guardians and her school. I was fed and clothed under the Sinclair roof, and there was always a nanny and she, whilst never a friend, was never quite an enemy. But the trouble was that Charlotte and I spoke a different language, dependent as we were upon different values and aspirations. We were oil and water, Left and Right. . . .

I felt dead. I felt that I was overseeing all this from another realm. Yet, even if I had so wished, I could not find adequate excuses for Charlotte. She had stood by and benefited from my rejection in the past and inheritance in the present. However, I was making her nervous; she saw that I had overcome the impediments of the past. The ritual duties she performed might seem less substantial to her now than they had a few hours ago.

Would I, when I got home, be able to unpack the canvas bag? Into my mind there floated the image of the wives of men who die in prison, who are summoned to the prison gates to take possession of the watch, the suit of clothing in which their husband was arrested, the two pounds and five pence found in his pocket, his dirty handkerchief, the wallet containing the photographs of his children. Of what possible solace could these objects be? I had always felt myself a prisoner of my ancestry. I had always known that Power cannot recognize Truth.

'They used to say that your posture was a reflection of your attitude to life.'

'Yes, they did. Funny that you should remember that.' I wondered what outward sign of selfishness, narcissism, snobbism and cruelty I might have detected from my mother's posture, and what weakness, arrogance and failed sexuality from my father's.

'I suppose the plain fact is that if only you could accept that some parents don't like their children, or one of their children, you'd be a great deal happier. You were hard to like, Antonia. I know it may sound cruel to say so, but there it is. And it isn't as if they made any bones about it. You can't accuse them of having misled you. They were not hypocritical. Anyhow, that's all water under the bridge now. You're a great success in your work. Father's dead, Mother's dying. I really can't understand why you seem so obsessed with the past.'

'Miss Sinclair! Miss Sinclair!' The nurse's voice was raised as she burst into the drawing-room. Charlotte followed her quickly up the stairs. This interruption had come at the right moment for me. Any more of Charlotte's *de haut en bas* tone and I might have lost my cool completely.

'Miss Sinclair has asked me to tell you that she will be no more than five minutes, and then you should prepare to go up to Mrs Sinclair's room.' I had not noticed the return of the nurse. I was surprised that I found her presence intrusive and that I resented her words.

Mother was plucking at the bed-cover. From time to time she groaned. Her face was ochre. I wondered whether this was the effect of the bedside light? It was not; she was seriously jaundiced and I had failed to notice this before. I looked at her more closely. Her jet-black hair had no grey in it. She had a faint moustache. She was hideous! I was sickened by the sight of her. Thank God I was not obliged to see beneath the bed-cover. I stood at the foot of the bed. I did not want to say anything to her; or touch her. In a way I should have liked to tell her that Walter and I had been lovers for many years. But my conscience would not have allowed me to deal her that blow. I should have liked, too, to tell her that she had burned her hatred into me with every malicious word and every slap, kick, pinch and trouncing she had administered herself or ordered Father to administer. But she was dying, and I was going to live on. Nor would I hang around for the threnody. I was not going in for that! Please God, Mother's passing will end all the pain. I had forgotten, at the time, that it was only with my return to the house, some seven hours past, that the pain had returned.

I left Mother to die in Charlotte's company. Charlotte told me emphatically that it was my duty to wait until the final throes. When I asked her why, she said it was the right thing. Walter used to say *Denn alle Schuld rächt sich auf Erden* – All guilt is punished on earth. Walter was wrong! Goethe was wrong! Mother had got away with it. Father had got away with it. There was to be no Nuremberg trial for them.

In my profession, only imagination and enthusiasm can illumine the craft skills of excavation and classification. I was accustomed to making greater and greater efforts to develop both. But in the present situation – such a personal one – I found myself desisting. Perhaps it was fear; but I did not wish to be further involved. I knew, too, that any attempts to cast light on the dark corners would be interpreted by my sister as evidence that I had no respect for the dead.

As I took down my jacket and picked up the canvas bag, I was haunted by the image of the worms that would eat their way out of Mother's body. I could not imagine Mother as pure spirit, nor could I imagine her as nothing. As I opened the front door and closed it behind me for all time, I said to myself: 'There is nothing to be afraid of!' And I shuddered.

Walter

Since yesterday I'm in love, presumably for a long time
to come. I love – a thirteen-year-old child. . . . Eleven
years ago I carried her in my arms. . . . Never . . . have I
felt my heart beat quite so anxiously and fast.

> 1.10.1886 Theodore Herzl, Diary

He cometh into the room like the morning sun.

> Song of Songs

IT WAS PAST MIDNIGHT. THE TEMPTATIONS OF PUBLIC TRANSPORT
were not open to me; there was no alternative but to walk back to
Camden Town. I felt more than exhausted: in a state of inanition. I
wandered unsteadily down the path towards the drive, but before
the gates were within sight I turned off on the path that led to the
summer-house.

I tried the door, meaning to force it if I had to, but found that
Madge had left the key in the lock. I pulled out a deck-chair and
sank into it. Everything smelt familiarly of damp canvas and wood.
A crystalline silence enveloped me.

They were all dead now. All dead – bar Charlotte. It would be
encouraging if, with the death of Mother, the death of her values
would follow. But that would be to ignore Charlotte. . . . At least
she had no children to bring low or inculcate. She and I were both
childless: the end of the line. We had both inherited the consequences of our parents' emotional inadequacy.

> Man hands on misery to man.
> It deepens like a coastal shelf.
> Get out as early as you can,
> And don't have any kids yourself.

'I'm going to have an abortion! That's final. There's no point in trying to stop me. I mean it. I'm going to ring Barbara at home this evening. She'll know what I should do. She'll know someone . . .'

'*Liebchen* . . .'

'Please, Walter . . . I beg you. Just don't.'

He has known me all my life, it makes it easy for him to assume a position of authority over me. But up to now it is something he has never tried to impose. I am dazzled by Walter: he is so confident. And because he severed all ties with Mother, I feel doubly safe.

It was 1951. I was twenty-one. Walter and I had been lovers for some months but I had waited until I came of age to move into the flat over his shop. Then I could do so legally, sustaining my financial independence and avoiding the inevitable tussle with Mother. In the event, Mother did not find it altogether surprising or unsuitable that I was 'taking a room' at Walter's place. I heard her say to Charlotte that, given available alternatives (she was thinking of my political contacts), she found it a quite sensible solution. She had never been up into the flat, she had no curiosity about Walter's way of life since she had relinquished her lien on it. She had paid fleeting visits to the bookshop on her way to or from engagements that involved her passing through a neighbourhood she would otherwise have taken steps to avoid, and she had put Walter in touch with refugee acquaintances wishing to dispose of foreign books and periodicals. Her charity work brought her into contact with people who did not read literary journals and who, therefore, missed the advertisements Walter placed in them.

After the war, when he was demobbed, Walter set himself up to acquire libraries for the Modern Languages departments of English-speaking universities throughout the world. Before the war he had had no regular, gainful employment. Now that he was naturalized and a veteran, he was as poor as Job. Mother had withdrawn her support from the day confirmation of Father's death reached her, saying that from that moment her resources had become over-stretched. They had not – or not seriously so. It was her need for Walter that had snapped.

'Just listen to me, *Liebchen!*' Unusually for him, Walter is blustering. 'We'll move out of Camden Town. We'll find some-where in the country. I'll work harder.' He is trying everything. It would be feasible to run the business from outside London. It does not matter from what address he issues his catalogues. It might even be better to settle somewhere in the middle of England because it would be easier to get to the north and Scotland. As for the benefits to our child: fresh air, farm food. . . . 'He'll grow up in three languages to the strains of Mozart and bird-song.'

I do not manage so much as a smile. While Walter lays plans stretching well into his son's adulthood, I lay plans to abort my daughter.

'But why? Why?'

'Well, I never got any parenting so I'd make a thoroughly inadequate parent myself. That's why.'

'So! Lisa and George are to exult in a final victory!'

Where had I found the strength to assert myself at a moment of such vulnerability?

In the very early days after Walter had told me he was in love with me, I was held in thrall by everything he thought and felt. I was eighteen and a student. By day I was studying and by night accompanying a group of socialists sorting out the Mosley thugs in the East End. I was a committed Zionist. I planned to emigrate to Israel once I had acquired the skills to put to the service of that new country. But as soon as Walter held me in an adult embrace and said 'I love you', everything changed. Only Walter mattered. The expression 'I love you' fell on me like the sound of the final chord in a long piece of music as it returns to the key in which it set out, but accompanied by many subtleties of expression accumulated along the way. I knew that nothing would ever be the same again. At first I was filled with a sense of relief and anxiety: relief that now all was revealed; anxiety that, the obvious having been acknowledged, there was nothing further to reveal. It was only after Walter died that it occurred to me that because there had been no one – no one at all – to watch us falling in love, there was no one to reassure me that the whole thing was not a dream.

Instantaneously I was struck by how lack-lustre were my university tutors. I had looked to them for wisdom and found mere skill. And my boy-friends, too, those with whom I patrolled the streets made unsafe for Jewish residents and round whose kitchen tables I sat, watching real mothers prepare real food. Walter's penetrating vision shone into every corner of my life. He encouraged my studies, but for their own sake. The acquisition of knowledge, he explained, was neither a proviso for social acceptance, as it seemed to Mother, nor an open sesame to the world of academe, as it seemed to my tutors, but a unique and privileged pleasure: an open window on the world.

'*"Der Zweck des Lebens ist das Leben selbst."* Life's not a testing-ground, it's not a competitive sport. It's a gift for which to be daily grateful and to celebrate.'

Now we would do together for all time in an adult way what we had done when I was an unhappy child.

Walter did not insist that I stop my political activities. He simply described to me from personal experience what real fascism involves. He ridiculed Mosley and his thugs, and made me feel I was spending my time brandishing a chopstick for a gun – and trying to build the temple at Bassai out of Lego.

'He's not worth your time and your attention. Just look at him. A little strutting rook! And his supporters. I bet you he never entertains any of them for so much as a cup of tea, let alone a weekend at his country place. No! He's been abandoned by all but a clutch of the mindless, a few hundred poor men and women with an axe to grind. If someone came along and offered each of them a hundred pounds to put in a post office savings account, Mosley would never see them again. The Duke's in exile, the appeasers are dead – or just buried. And it's positively *un*fashionable to be anti-Semitic these days.'

I am not merely inconvenienced by the discovery that I am pregnant, I am livid. I have taken odious precautions and they have let me down. Have I not consulted that top birth-control specialist in London? Did I not permit her to examine me and fit me with a cap? Have I not armed myself with tubes of sperm-killing substances? And did I not take to heart with religious fervour the grim warning of what would happen if I left the cap in its tin in my chest of drawers and the jelly beside it in its tube? Yet in spite of it all, the bloody thing has let me down! And now Walter's undermining my purpose by subjecting me to moral blackmail.

'But *Liebchen*, this is *our* child.'

I wonder, now, did Walter have some presentiment of his early death, some intimation that made it especially urgent for him to find his life prolonged in another's? I can still see his face creased in agony, still hear the weird sighs that accompanied his pleas: 'Is there to be no legacy of our love?'

'We looked; we loved and therewith instantaneously Death became terrible to you and me.'

'Barbara?' I explain that the GP says he will support me but the law requires his support to be backed by a certificate from a psychiatrist. Dear Barbara, I have not spoken to her for ages but I know I can rely on her. (Had Albrecht Kurtz been alive, he would no doubt have taken the keenest pleasure in testifying to my complete unsuitability for child-rearing on the grounds of my mental instability and 'possession'.)

'Dr Hamilton-Barnes deals out certificates with the agility of a croupier,' she assures me, as she turns up his address and telephone number. 'Make an appointment to see him some time next week! In the meantime, I'll ring him and soften him up. And let me know how it goes. Good luck.'

I replace the receiver, hugely relieved. Barbara has the quality of empathy I need. She is enlightened and has progressive views.

Dr Hamilton-Barnes is extravagantly well turned out. He makes some pretence of taking down my psychiatric history, but I have the feeling that he does this only to give his solid gold fountain-pen an airing. He agrees that an unmarried woman of twenty-five embarking on an academic career (not much money in that, is there?) would be foolish to interrupt it by going ahead with an unwanted pregnancy, occasioned by an impecunious refugee twenty-four years her senior.

'A book-dealer?' His eyebrows hoist themselves. 'Polish, Hungarian, Romanian!' He is aghast. 'I didn't know those chaps wrote books.' He folds the certificate and slips it into an envelope.

'Well,' I answer politely, counting twenty-five guineas on to his desk, 'a lot of the material he buys is French and German.'

I wonder why I imagine that information lends a degree of respectability to Walter's occupation? Why do I feel the need to come to his defence?

The abortion proved to be a watershed in my life. I was manifestly no longer a child now, no longer an adolescent. I was a woman, and Walter was disturbed by my fierce display of independence and haunted by the spectre of losing me altogether. He insisted that a child would not only crown our love but sanctify it. It occurred to me that what he was yearning for was a child in whom to go on loving the child that had been me. And yearning, too, to find me subdued in motherhood.

Where had I found the strength to assert myself? I tried to remember. I looked towards the house. The lights were still burning in the drawing-room and on the first-floor landing. I wondered whether Charlotte was weeping. I wondered whether the nurse had intimate things to do with Mother's body.

It was Walter who lent me his skills of judgement as a tool with which I was to discover my own. This fired me with the determination to assert myself definitively over the abortion: I owed it to Walter's wisdom as much as to my own self-respect.

Since seeing Dr Hamilton-Barnes I have rung Barbara again and invited her to supper. It isn't long into the meal before I become conscious that Walter is not talking much. I feel a little uncomfortable. Clearly Barbara is not his type – too English, I imagine. It is her Englishness that I find so reassuring. She has a way of moving as if she were being pulled along by a large dog on a stout lead. But I find everything about Barbara reassuring. For example, she has not changed; she belongs to a community of English women who do not change, in physical appearance, to accommodate the passing of time; or their growing reputations. She is a constant. Furthermore, she has imbued me with a passion for French painting. Whereas the walls at home were plastered with valuable works of art that gave me no joy, Barbara's desk is filled with postcards of paintings I pore over. They give me an indelible sense of well-being. There are Bonnards and Sisleys and Pissarros in whose fields, along whose waterways, over whose hills I roamed imaginatively from seven years of age – and still roam. And Vuillards whose domestic intimacies arouse in me a nostalgia for something I long for but have never experienced. And Barbara has taught me to cook fairy cakes and fudge. And she encourages me to listen carefully to recordings of Schubert's and Schumann's piano music.

I know I am taking the right action or Barbara would not be supporting me.

'I don't think we met when Antonia was little,' Barbara says as she eats the avocado pear I have stuffed with a spiced crabmeat filling. 'Of course I used to hear a lot about you.'

I suppose I spoke of Walter as the author of treats, particularly those aborted by Mother on the grounds of some recent misdemeanour of which I was guilty.

'No,' Walter replies to the first remark, ignoring the second altogether and rising to go into the kitchen for the Tabasco sauce he thinks my filling lacks. Barbara was party to something Walter maintains was not only objectively wrong but personally wounding. It is not surprising that he does not welcome my accomplice with much warmth.

'I shall be accompanying Antonia to the nursing home myself. I shall wait by her bed until she is well enough to be moved, when I shall bring her home. She will rest for as long as it takes, and then I shall take her away somewhere. She'll need the sun.' Walter is pretending that he is none the less in control.

We have finished supper. Walter suggests that Barbara and I might prefer to talk privately. Meanwhile he will attend to the dishes. However, before this suggestion is put into action, and as we hover between the kitchen and the sitting-room, mugs of coffee in our hands, Walter starts haranguing the various medical specialists involved in our present situation: general practitioners, psychiatrists, surgeons. They may do their worst for this occasion, but he will see to it personally that they are subsequently returned to their murky world under some stone or other.

'It's a scandal that these quacks make money out of other people's tragedies!'

When Barbara and I finally escape into the sitting-room and Walter closes the door behind us, I explain how Hamilton-Barnes charged twenty-five guineas, insisting he had to 'cover' himself, and how the abortionist, an unprepossessing GP with a practice in Ealing and a nursing home in his wife's name, was demanding three hundred pounds to 'cover' himself.

'Abortion will have to be legalized.' Barbara is adamant. 'If for no other reasons than to make it safe and to stop these dreadful people from coining money. But just this once, you're in their hands – and at their mercy.'

Yes, I agree. I am particularly anxious not to sound ungrateful to Barbara, who has saved my life.

We start to talk of old times, and as we do so the irony of the present situation is borne in on me. My very existence, since just before I was sent to Barbara as a patient, has been predicated on a falsehood: I did not commit the act that led to the damage inflicted on my life and I resent being implicated in atrocities committed against me. But had I not been the butt of my parents' inadequacies and their conflict, I might never have returned Walter's passion for me – or become pregnant by him. The image of a skein of fine fibres terminating in a single gold thread – our requited love – steals into my mind. But I am also aware that there is something incestuous about this love. I feel that its issue will necessarily have to be sacrificed. While Barbara talks me back into the past, the abiding pall of lonely fear wraps itself closely about me.

I am relieved to be wrenched back into the present when Walter pushes through the door with more coffee. I get up and take a cup for Barbara and one for myself.

'All done!' He is triumphant, and I thank him. I kiss him on both cheeks. I hope to lighten the atmosphere that has turned dull and mistrustful. Unfortunately, however, Walter asks what we have been talking about, and hearing that it has been my childhood, he starts to interrogate Barbara about the drama of the cut clothes. Who did she think responsible at the time? Has she changed her mind since?

'It was not my job to track down the culprit,' Barbara tells him, adding that she is quite sure it wasn't me. She says that not only were there practical reasons why it was impossible for me to have done what I was accused of – 'She was terrified of the dark and never left her room at night to go down to the floor below. No scissors were ever found, no ink . . .' – but she never found any evidence in my talk and play to link me with the incident. 'It could have been a servant,' she continues. She takes a long draught of coffee before elaborating. 'You know, some young girl up from the country, finding herself in awe of her mistress's wealth and social standing, desiring to be noticed, appreciated, and above all associated with her – needing to oust any competition for attention. She may have judged that the route to her employer's heart was over Antonia's dead body. There may even have been an element of sexual desire on her part – unrequited, unobserved. . . .'

While Barbara fleshes it out, I cringe from this scenario. What subordinate could possibly have felt that way towards Mother, who in any case would have shown nothing but icy contempt for her? On the other hand, I remember how Mother always adopted a peculiarly virulent hostility towards homosexuals; and she had a marked tendency to sadism. Had she an unresolved problem? Had she been tempted by some young lass offering herself to be used in exchange for adoration? Had she rejected her brusquely and without kindliness, and set the scene for what ensued? It was an intriguing idea.

'Do you remember if there were any very young maids in your mother's service at the time?' Barbara asks.

I do not. Looking back I remember Nanny, who always seemed old, and Cook. And Mrs Rudge the charwoman.

'I doubt that it was your father,' Barbara continues thoughtfully. 'I can't see what he would have got out of it.'

Walter cuts in. Could it have been, he wonders, that George needed an excuse to chastise Antonia particularly severely at a time when he had no other way to placate his wife? Knowing Lisa's attachment to her finery, he may have calculated that the destruction of several articles of clothing would provide the perfect excuse to beat the daylights out of the culprit.

'That does sound rather far-fetched, Walter!' I am laughing.

But Walter knew Father as a peer. I never did. I shudder to think of the machinations of my parent's mind. Walter is describing to Barbara Father's stilted manner and his abhorrence of any type of demonstration of affection.

'An icy man . . . unfulfilled . . . a joyless individual. The sort who knows how to survive with a penknife in the jungle. He could have put up a tent in a hurricane on a mountainside and lit a fire with sodden wood. All very fine, but such men rarely know how to respond to women.'

I look up at Walter. I know that he means more than he is saying.

'Or children,' Barbara adds.

I resolve to think about Walter's relations with Father later.

'I was struck at the time that none of Lisa's most expensive, prized evening clothes were attacked. Of course I didn't draw attention to this. I felt in my bones that it wouldn't be prudent to comment on the vandal's selectivity. Lisa showed me cut and stained blouses and unravelled knitwear. I remember there was some torn satin underwear. . . . But the lavishly beaded and embroidered evening silks weren't touched.'

'Are you saying that Mrs Sinclair herself was responsible?'

'No. But I am saying that it seemed possible at the time.'

There is a pause and then Walter says: 'Mrs Sinclair's a more complex woman than she appears. She's not particularly intelligent, and she's never been able to accept her limitations and make the best of what she's capable of. She burns with frustration, she feels thwarted. It may be out of those feelings that she's developed an instinct for knowing how to manipulate situations for her own ends. It's those ends that have been hard to fathom.'

'Do you think she knew precisely what they were?' I ask Walter.

'No. What she thought she wanted was not what she really yearned for. But she'd taken a decision, "made her bed" as the English put it. She'd acquired a well-born Englishman, vetted and approved by her papa. She'd lashed herself to the mast of social acceptance, and her resolve was to keep tight the bonds that secured – and thwarted – her.'

Barbara is clearly disinclined to expand upon this subject, and I fill an awkward silence by asking her whether she remembers how Albrecht Kurtz and Mother conceived the notion that I was possessed by the devil. Barbara laughs. I think yes, it is laughable, in a way, but I notice that Walter is not laughing.

'Lisa's a Manichean *manqué*. She's programmed psychologically to see everything in terms of black and white, right and wrong, good and bad. She's always been unsuited to procedures that are mind-expanding. She's never had the guts to look into the sources of her convictions – prejudices would be a more apt term. It certainly ill-behoved her to regard you as "Darkness" redeemable only by reconciliation to the Bergner-Sinclair "Light". And I may say, I never regarded Lisa and George as *boni homines*.'

Walter is wound up. He is sweating. I don't know quite what to do or say to diffuse the situation. I can tell that Barbara feels uneasy. She seems not to trust Walter.

'Did your sister have a motive for getting you into hot water?' she asks.

'She didn't need to. She was the favourite child.'

'Of course she had every reason, *Liebchen*. She was consumed with jealousy of you.'

Walter relates to Barbara how, some months past, Mother came into the bookshop with Charlotte, and how Charlotte engaged him in formal conversation while Mother made a protracted telephone call. Charlotte explained that she was engaged in a project designed to make professional Asians feel more at home in Britain. She confided to Walter that it was hard to be a foreigner in Britain and she was most fortunate to have been born here. Walter wondered why Charlotte found it appropriate to tell *him* that.

'I can remember Charlotte at seven. She was already middle-aged. I have no doubt but that she was programmed for spinster-dom. She walked as if she had one of her father's batons down her spine. She wore a permanent expression of disdain on her face, and if I asked her a question she would answer wordlessly, with an enigmatic smile or a toss of the head. She almost invariably refused to speak to me, even as a very young child. And she knew full well that I found this unnerving. When she was a little older, she would practise being rude to me behind Lisa's and George's backs. Of course she was frantic with jealousy of all the attention I paid to Antonia. Looking back, I've wondered if she sensed, somehow, what the future would bring. I know she always had the effect of making me feel guilty.'

And now it is Walter's litany of my perfections that embarrasses me. I leave the room, quietly. They will both think I am heading for the bathroom.

I stare into the looking-glass on my dressing-table. This is the woman that Walter loves. There is nothing about me that he does not accept. That is to say, there was nothing. I know that I am right to go ahead with the abortion but I am astonished that I am able so to violate his feelings.

It was not surprising that the first man to whom I gave myself was Walter. He was the only man with whom I could lose my separateness without losing what was left of my identity. My sense of self was frail, and closely connected to my suffering. At first it was disorientating to be loved unconditionally, to be believed and not to be abused verbally or physically. My parents had always regarded with suspicion at best, and derision at worst, what I thought and what I did.

I had always had a problem in taking decisions: was I really right in the action I proposed, would the consequences be as I predicted? More often than not I avoided pitfalls by avoiding action. Then, suddenly, there was Walter day and night, taking it for granted that what I thought and what I did was good, right and even commendable. I waited for a display of rage, for the expression of contempt – at least for a measure of moodiness. But I waited in vain. Walter was even-tempered, and whatever I said or did brought him pleasure. I did not have to strive to please him, he was glad simply to have me at his side.

'George was a weak man. That's why he was so inflexible and why he had to protect his image so zealously.'

So that was it! And Walter, being strong, could be undemanding, compliant, tractable and accessible. With him I caught a glimpse of the other side of the sun.

'He may have exercised his will at work but it was Lisa's he exercised at home.'

Walter only ever wanted my happiness. Indeed he repeatedly insisted that I should demand nothing less and that I should be more courageous in taking up arms against anyone and any situation that threatened to deprive me of it. I never admitted to him that I was incapable of the unalloyed happiness he wanted for me. He would have regarded such an admission as reflecting poorly on himself: he thought he was some sort of magician who could wipe out the damage of the past and re-create life in the present. He refused to see that the present was nothing but layer upon layer of what went before – sugared perhaps, rearranged perhaps, and certainly glazed over. He dared not.

Since we had been lovers there were questions I had wanted to put to him. What, for example, was the relationship between Mother and him? Why had he never married? Had he loved me only because I was Mother's child?

'I never thought of you as Lisa's child. . . .'

It was only when I became pregnant with Walter's child that I wondered whether, when I was a child, he had loved in me what he had loved in Mother when she was little.

Walter told me that the serene bliss of our love for one another – our passion roused and gratified, and our quotidian life – had succeeded in overcoming our separateness in the present, and no shadows from the past could come between us. I believed that beneath the polished surface of present time, the layers of stained, distressed and worm-eaten years could be revealed by a mere scratch of a finger-nail. My pregnancy, my abortion, was proof.

Walter has come into the bedroom for Barbara's coat.

'Your friend's leaving.'

I follow Barbara down the narrow stairs to the front door.

'Incidentally, I'm sorry I had to spill the beans to Hamilton-Barnes, but I had to explain our relationship. All I said was that you'd come to me for play therapy following "an unresolved schizoid episode". You know that's not what I actually believe, but it was what I felt I had to say to clinch the deal.' Barbara pats my arm: 'I'm sorry, Antonia, that this old business still shadows you.'

Indeed it does, I think, as I open the front door and then close it gently behind her. And I'm sorry too. My whole childhood is crystallized in an event at which I did not assist. I cannot make out which is worse: being convicted of something of which I was innocent or being punished for something for which, had I been guilty, I should have received double doses of care and understanding. As I mount the stairs I realize that however much Walter tries to confirm me, I shall never be able wholly to incorporate the sense of my worth that he reflects. For me to be able to be truly myself in the presence of another would have required a mother with whom, as an infant, I could have been alone without anxiety.

The lights were still on in the house and the full moon bathed the garden in colourlessness. Could it be said that a rose was red or only that, lent light, it was red? I pulled the holdall towards me and unzipped it. I removed Mr Bear and held him to my face. His soft fur and peculiar scent reminded me . . . oddly, not of hurt and shame, but of something ineffably consoling. Mr Bear and I were closely related. He was, and was not, me.

I believe I know when I conceived. I take pains not to confide this to Walter because otherwise he will become even more hostile to the idea of abortion: there is something affecting about knowing just when the sperm has met the egg and been accepted by it. I conceal from him, too, the astonishing experience I had at the moment of conception.

It is a Sunday. We always lie in on Sundays. When we wake up we see that the sky is overcast and rain is tumbling silently from low clouds. We agree that nothing would be nicer than to stay where we are, with the papers and breakfast on trays. Time passes without our noticing it. One or other of us gets up to replenish cups and plates and find more reading material and it is only when the street lights are shining, in the special way they do when it is raining, that we notice it is late afternoon. The music critic who lives in the flat above the bakery next door has been playing different versions of *Rosenkavalier* all day and we rejoice in the good fortune of having such a neighbour rather than one devoted to music that is only noise to our ears. I notice in *The Observer* that *Brief Encounter* is on at the Everyman and we consider getting up and going to the final showing, but we never make it. Walter goes to bathe but, instead of dressing, comes back to bed and gathers me into his arms to make love.

I am feeling unusually tired and wonder why this should be. I relax in the aroma of his sandalwood-scented embrace and then, at the moment at which he penetrates me, I feel myself leave my body. I find myself floating just below the ceiling of the bedroom, watching Walter's body covering my own on our double bed. I am struck by the luxuriance of his shining black hair and slim, lithe body. The thought crosses my mind that I am being loved by Walter twenty years earlier. . . . I look out of the window to my immediate right, to the opposite side of the street, into the lighted rooms of the terrace houses. I see that the couple who live over their paper shop are taking tea. They are seated round a white-painted table, the top of which is concealed under newspapers.

I do not feel myself drop back down into my body crushed beneath that of Walter's. I do not feel anything very odd has happened to me – not even an altered state of consciousness – and it is not until many years later that I learn that out-of-body experiences are quite common and that many people who experience them shy away from talking about them.

'Women can become very depressed after an abortion. It's a sort of death, you know, and you'll grieve,' Walter warns, going on to say that because there is no formal ceremony to expiate the grief, the consequences are often painful and debilitating. But we are on our way to Ealing. The die is cast.

Walter informs the nurse that, since he is paying for the abortion (not strictly true), he feels free to insist, against her instruction, on staying with me before the operation and being there when I come round. No, he will not leave! Nothing in the world could convince him that my best interests would be served by his leaving.

At the time this conversation is taking place, I am in bed, waiting for the injection that will relax me before I am wheeled into the operating theatre. Walter sits hunched, fingering the frayed arms of the claret-coloured, cut-moquette Parker Knoll chair – the only chair in the room.

'The wife's certainly not got much in the way of taste,' he observes, his eyes scanning skimpy curtains, stained carpet and a much-scratched beechwood chest of drawers. Pointing to the wallpaper, he says he is reminded of rampant acne. Then, drawing his finger along the window-sill, he comments on the flagrant absence of cleanliness.

There seems nothing else for us to talk about, we who are never at a loss.

Walter gets up and peers out of the window. 'It's a fire-escape,' he informs me, evoking in me the image of miserable women in nightdresses, clutching whatever they can lay hands on, making fast escapes. 'I can count fifteen galvanized dustbins in the yard. It's concreted,' he continues sadly. 'We can guess what goes into them.'

Hic iacet pulvis cinis et nihil.

I keep my eyes fixed on Walter and feel overwhelming tenderness for him. He is a brave man. I have never heard him complain about his circumstances. I have never seen him give in to them. There is absolutely nothing shoddy about him. He makes himself responsible for himself. He washes and irons his shirts with the expertise of a Chinese laundress. He polishes his shoes so that without their appearing newly acquired, they never look neglected. He sees to it that his only suit, expensive and well-fitting, is clean and pressed. In the years between the end of the war and my coming to live with him, I had felt the vulnerability beneath the efforts to maintain appearances. Since moving in with him and watching his perseverance, I have been deeply touched. Everything about Walter has a particular kind of fastidiousness.

When I was a child I did not notice his accent. Whereas Mother had had a French governess when she was little, Walter had had an English one. Whereas Mother's English was laced with far too many z's and much gargling in the throat, Walter's was lighter. The army did the rest. Walter's charm and knowledge earned him a cushy number as batman to the colonel, a cultivated if lazy Eton-educated Jew who, in exchange for Walter's talking to him frequently and at length about Goethe (Walter's most passionate preoccupation at the time), helped Walter to expunge the errant v's and drag his r's out of his windpipe to the roof of his mouth. Now, I notice, I find his speaking voice as alluring as his appearance. Nevertheless, I beg him to go home and work and return only when the doctor says it is safe for me to be moved. He refuses; he will read and sleep in the chair until I am ready to dress and leave. He will go out for something to eat while I am 'being done'.

It was only following long periods away from Mother, during the war, that her English offended and shocked me when I heard it. It was not that it was ungrammatical – and it had range – but it was unreliable and when she became excited, which was not infrequently, she would revert to stringing words together, a linguistic opportunity provided for by the German but not the English language. However, since those days it was evident that her means of expression – its tone and colour – had been influenced by her proximity to Charlotte. What it lacked in originality it had gained in welcome conformity.

When I come round, back in the horrid, dirty little room, I hear Walter asking the nurse what sex the child would have been.

Walter closed the shop, paid all the outstanding bills and took me into the sun to recuperate. As it happened I felt fine; an inconvenience had been lifted from me and I could get on with life again. Walter, however, did not look well and was decidedly less communicative than usual. It occurred to me that he might be worried about money.

We ambled through France on B roads almost entirely devoid of traffic. There were any number of villages that I would have been happy to settle in, particularly one or two in the Massif Central, but Walter was heading for Spain. There was a priest in Alicante who had an ancient text he might be persuaded to dispose of. Walter had a client interested in acquiring it and so I did not demur.

We found a village – no more than a hamlet – hung on a hill that rose straight out of rocky beach near Alicante. The only *fondas* was built into the cliff about a hundred feet above the shore. We were shown into a whitewashed room with a double bed with an elaborately carved headboard. The other furnishings, if one could call them that, were a fruitwood cross that hung immediately opposite the bed, and a poster showing a small bull and a large matador. The windows of the room overlooked the sea. We were the sole visitors at the *fondas*. Indeed, the inn seemed so empty, it was hard to imagine there had been other visitors in living memory.

We spent much of our time reading, talking or just watching the sea from the vine-clad terrace. It was here that the *patróna de pensión* served us saffron-scented paellas, freshly caught grilled *calamares* and *sardinas*, and baskets of *uvas* and *melocoton* – and so much wine that we were almost perpetually drowsy.

In the late afternoon we would stroll into the village. There was not much of it, just a tiny whitewashed church with a bell that sounded the hours and half a dozen maize- and apricot-coloured houses, their stucco peeling encircling a dusty square, at the centre of which stood a waterless fountain with a cracked basin. Women who caught sight of us from behind their windows would emerge to water the bright geraniums they grew in used olive-oil tins at their doorways. Occasionally the men in black who sat in the café playing dominoes would look up to see whose feet were stirring the sandy dust. We would murmur *buenas tardes* and pass on in the direction of the lane that led out on to the hill and the hobbled donkey.

Around eleven o'clock at night, the *patron* returned from his olive grove. After exchanging sign language with him, we would move down the steps that led to the shore, and by the light of the moon – and sometimes by the light of the phosphorus lamps on the fishing-boats – take a last swim before going to bed.

After it was over, I was left with a sense of rapture. Our isolation was made complete there in Spain, and we relished it. Walter celebrated my body with a sort of religious fervour.

'My beloved is mine and I am his.' We are at peace. There is no one to disturb us. 'A bundle of myrrh is my well-beloved unto me; he shall lie all night betwixt my breasts.' The heat of the day is such that it never disperses, and throughout the night the air in our room remains thick and hot. We adhere. His fruit has been sweet to my taste; my fruit has been sweet to his. We have explored one another's bodies in their most secret places and have murmured that 'it is fair . . . without blemish'. Walter clings to me for a long time. He has satisfied his desire more quickly than he wished and has stayed covering my body with his own.

'You ravish my heart,' he says. 'Your breath tastes of honey, your hair smells of dried grasses, your skin is smooth as rose petals. . . .'

Drunk with satisfaction, he falls silent. I too am beyond words. I feel for his hand and clasp it, conscious that his fingers know more of me than I know of myself. I am grateful for the blue-black dark that envelops us. Shortly, I feel him stir again. He fastens his mouth over my breast. A sharp thrill stabs me and I moan. 'Beautiful! Beautiful!' he responds, as he heaves his body across mine again, pushes his thigh between my legs and separates them wide.

Inside, like an aroused sea anemone, I fold round his sex.

As the sun rises, the crickets sing and the cock crows, and we go down to the sea. We are alone in a soundless world. Hand in hand, we walk until the gently fretting waters cover my shoulders. Cool at last!

'Love is as strong as death,' he whispers.

With my arms I clasp him round the neck and with my legs I clasp him round the waist: crablike. 'Live for ever!' I demand. 'Never leave me!' I insist. I am sick with love. Never leave me . . . I hear the echo and I feel the terror: one day this idyll will end. Down, down I descend into the world of darkness and perpetual solitude. In my mind's eye I see the black cloud that carries away the sun.

Walter had stopped smarting over the abortion somewhere in mid-France, and for the first time I found it possible to ask him about his early life and, in particular, his relations with Mother and Father.

When Lisa – my mother – was a child she was different from the other children his parents arranged for him to play with, nor was she like his brothers. Those children did no more than fulfil roles assigned to them by their social circumstances. Mother, on the other hand, was something of a tomboy, a rebel. She and Walter were *Kameraden*. There was a little island on the lake in the grounds of Schloss Huberman, where Walter played Man Friday to Mother's Robinson Crusoe. When they grew up and had access to money, they planned to run away to the South Seas.

'Perhaps it was our sense of security', Walter said, 'that made it possible for us to indulge in fantasies. But I believe this treasure-island play nurtured seeds already sown in Lisa's imagination. She always determined to live abroad – certainly not in a wattle hut, though. She wanted something beyond imagination. She loved her father dearly, but rejected altogether the plans he was laying for her future. As an adolescent she had wanted to study music. Her father faced the signs of her artistic ambitions with alarm, insisting that it was hard to find a man to marry a woman with a vocation. It was a long time before Lisa understood what her father meant. She didn't have the remotest idea of what was involved in the pursuit of the artistic life. Old Bergner paid his daughter the compliment of steering her clear of a life for which she was demonstrably unsuited.

But, subsequently, the failure to become a musician surely poisoned her existence. It was made worse because she married a man who played the piano so much better than she, and none the less chose an altogether different career. Lisa never developed the emotional maturity to become proficient in the arts.'

It was Grandfather Bergner who found Father for her. Grandfather met the Sinclairs in Vichy, where they were taking the waters. Broughton Sinclair was something of an eccentric, who enjoyed vexing his peers by outlandish pronouncements and behaviour. He had an abundance of history to his name but was shorter of funds than he would have liked. He saw the advantages of an alliance between a prosperous European Jewish woman and his youngest son, so long as the woman did not look 'too Jewish' and was prepared to turn up at church for weddings, christenings and funerals. My grandfather turned the matter over in his mind and found that he was not displeased. At the second offer of an invitation to the Sinclair seat, Saint Groats, he journeyed to England. On his return he announced himself well-satisfied. He too had a taste for early English silver, medieval oak and sixteenth-century portraiture. He too enjoyed a view of parkland studded with deer. In the event, my mother seemed to have been happy to make her father happy. She substituted for previous fantasies the vaguer idea of doing something 'different'. Marrying the youngest son of an English baronet combined doing differently with satisfying her father.

'But she was never in love with George. She never professed to be. She entered into this condition with her eyes wide open. She could never be accused of having married absent-mindedly. She chose what she considered to be "a dignified state of being, dependent upon rational and practical considerations". Those were her very words. But she achieved a misalliance. I once heard her criticize a married woman acquaintance for displaying signs of passion for her husband, saying it was vulgar, inappropriate to the married state. And I remember a conversation about arranged marriages – Lisa insisting they were an excellent convention, and George agreeing. Never mind that he was eventually made a brigadier, he was a weak man. He always had to be told what to do and what to think. I don't know what he really thought about anything. I only know that the step he never took was the one that took him out of step with Lisa. . . .'

While Walter was speaking, I remembered that all that Mother ever read was romantic fiction.

When I was small, I assumed that Walter lived in London, if I thought about it at all. I never wondered with whom, or where. Asking personal questions of adults was something I was taught not to do. It became second nature not to do so. The result of this was that Walter existed in my mind only in so far as he was with me. I never imagined his being married, in love, a father – or even surrounded by friends. It was not until we were in Spain together that I learnt something about his independent past.

During the 1930s he visited London frequently. Sometimes he stayed at our house, at other times with other people, and often in a service flat near Regent's Park. He always made a point of being in London for my birthday and for Christmas. It was not until the *Anschluss* that he moved permanently to England, and this he did without luggage – emotional or material. He told me that when I was about three or four, he arrived at the house to find George away and Lisa with too much time on her hands. She was clearly dissatisfied. After a number of false starts, she hinted that George fell short of accomplishment in the field of love-making. As she laboured to make her meaning clear, without using words she regarded as offensive, Walter realized that Mother had a dual purpose in confiding these details to him. Certainly she needed to talk (and do so in German), and who else was there to tell? But the more subtle reason was that she hoped to flatter Walter by showing up her husband's deficiencies.

'I felt sickened. I understood perfectly what she was up to. She thought that by confiding in me she would make me feel so intimate with her that I would reciprocate by confiding in her. I had kept my private life to myself for many years and this irritated her. Added to which, she wanted someone to pay court to her who was in no way a threat. Being vain, she pretended that there existed between us some sort of romantic attachment. She suggested that, had she married me, she would have known sexual fulfilment. But having married George, for the purposes of making an alliance, getting away from Germany, doing something different, she had paid the penalty of frustration. *Gar verdriesslich ist mir einsam das Lager zu Nacht*, she quoted, attempting a meaning from which I turned away. Lisa had no sensitivity to poetry but believed that by expressing her desire in the words of Goethe, a poet she knew I loved and respected, she disguised her lack of imagination and sweetened her purpose. I remember her adding, with a sigh: "We were not put on earth to be happy!" I can't tell you how much I resented her putting me on the spot like that. I'd never been in love with her. I'd never had the remotest desire to marry her. And had she been honest with herself – an option not really open to her – I was nothing more than a link with the past. The past for Lisa was a more agreeable country than the present. . . . The trouble was that when she looked back, she looked right back into the years of childhood when, it is true, we were inseparable, living a fantasy. She conveniently forgot the years between, when our paths seldom crossed. And, as I said, she was hell-bent on prising those years from me.

'Lisa never went back to Germany after '35, whereas I was coming and going right up to '38. We knew so many people in common, and places, and I brought her news first hand of what was going on. And there were the German chocolates and colognes she liked. . . . All that side of life, the German side, was something she couldn't share with George, and so my visits and our conversations must have had the effect of making him feel something of a stranger in his own house. Perhaps his reaction to this alien status was to get at me through his behaviour towards you.

'I admit it, the house was a convenient stopover. Lisa was living very well and the hospitality in the avenue was abundant. But I came to see you. I know how unusual it is for a young man to feel towards a child how I felt towards you. I know that George, for example, saw it as unnatural and said as much. I did love you in a very special way but there was nothing improper about it. I knew I had to wait. In the meantime I feared for you. I seemed to transfer my feelings for the vulnerable in Europe – for whom I could do nothing – to one small child in London. I thought that if I turned up from time to time, no one would dare to do you lasting harm. There would always be someone to ask difficult questions. I suppose I was thinking of lasting physical harm. But like most motives I admit that mine were mixed.'

After Walter admitted that his motives had been mixed, he paused long enough for me to consider whether it had been strictly normal for a grown man to have loved a friend's child so inordinately and to have waited for that child to become his adult lover. Of course there had been nothing abnormal about it all: unusual, perhaps. But Barbara had been suspicious. I realized that at the time but took pains to conceal it from myself. I could not bear her disapproval. Yet it was her disapproval that had made it easy for me to get the abortion. And on what grounds could she have possibly rejected Walter? I was an adult now. . . .

Walter talked on. 'I too liked going over the past,' he continued. 'But for me it was the past. I looked back on Baden-Baden and all that as if on a faded, sepia photograph. It was Lisa who always tried dragging things into the present. Perhaps I was guilty of encouraging her. Perhaps I felt that unless I allowed her to imagine she was implicating me, I would be less likely to receive her invitations. The real and actual world was something of a disappointment to Lisa. Ostensibly, she was infatuated with England, the British Army, the landed gentry and all the rest of it. But I don't think she believed in her heart that England, the British Army, landed gentry and so forth – with the possible exception of her father-in-law who connived with her and then died shortly after she and George married – were infatuated with her.

'She tried using me to keep George on his toes when you were little. Once George was dead, she had no further pressing need of me. But another reason for her making me redundant was that, once I was a refugee, I couldn't travel back and forth. I couldn't replenish her stocks of news and goodies. Being a refugee reduced me to a pitiable condition in her eyes, and then my being interned as an enemy alien on the Isle of Man hardly contributed to my status.'

Later, Walter was to reveal to me some of the details of his personal life and the source of his feelings of guilt. I could understand how awful he felt about the fate of his family because he had shared so little with them. But I did feel a bit upset when he told me about his friend Anna, and how she had aborted their child. I did not like the sense that somehow I had replaced that child in his affections.

It was during this conversation, when Walter confided in me how glad he had been to leave behind his complex personal life in Germany, that he finally emerged from the shadows of the past into the full glare of the present. He became more real for me: not merely a wonder-man, existing in a void with the sole purpose of providing me with succour, but someone with needs of his own. I was disturbed by much of what he told me. I felt pangs of jealousy, together with those of pain for his suffering, but I also found myself falling more and more in love with him as I faced the variety of his experiences. I was careful not to question him; I wanted to know only what he wanted to tell me. The story of Anna, the beautiful Aryan, who aborted his child for fear that it might look Jewish and implicate her and her family, made a deep impression on me. But I refused to allow myself to dwell on the implications this event had for our own experience. I saw that episode as one typical in the life of any European Jew. Similarly with his feelings of guilt. He was alive; his family was dead. This was something that all refugees had to cope with.

We wandered up and down the shore, strolled into the village and climbed into the hills. All the time Walter talked, I had the feeling that the few peasants we passed, unable to understand a word of what we said, none the less understood perfectly the unassailable intimacy between us, and this gave me profound satisfaction. And shored up my confidence.

Walter had had time and space in London in which to confide the details of his past, yet he had avoided doing so. He had needed to find a place unfamiliar to both of us where he could unburden himself, perform an autopsy – and an interment; a place to which we need never return. It was clear that in doing so he felt a sense of relief. He discovered that there was nothing he could not reveal to me, and I discovered that there was nothing that could come between us.

I did not tell Walter that I had been advised by the doctor not to make love for two months following the abortion. It was not merely that I did not want to disappoint him, I felt an urgent need for this expression, and we made love more often and with greater abandon than ever. Nothing in our love-making resembled anything else in our day-to-day routine. It was not so much affection that we expressed. After every coming together I felt I had been assisting in some rite of nature, some observance in which the hills, the forests, the earth and the sky were reflected. I was first drunk with desire and then somnolent with gratification. Walter, with all his personal past, would dissolve, and in place of him as an individual I experienced him as pure life-force. Our intercourse was dreamlike, and as I slowly awoke from the dream it took me several seconds to re-establish Walter as my man of qualities.

'Lisa and George never gave the impression of being a married couple, sharing intimacies. They seemed a couple of strangers, conspirators, who had chosen to live intermittently under the same roof. There was no real mutual regard between them. Nothing positive united them, merely dependence and recrimination, and their abuse of you. Of course George was often away. Lisa had made it clear from the start that she wasn't going to be the typical army wife, living wherever her husband was posted. "I don't care for packing and unpacking," she explained, disingenuously, since it would not have been Lisa who attended to either. I don't know how George managed it, but although he was frequently out of London it was never for very long. And it wasn't until war broke out that he was posted abroad. Lisa stayed put throughout the thirties. I rather imagine that something of their resentment of one another crystallized in Lisa's stubborn refusal not to budge and George's obligation to move around. Lisa has always had a marked appreciation of what she feels is owed to her. Maintaining the London house came high on her list of priorities.'

'A sound tree reproduces good fruit but a rotten tree bad fruit.' I was haunted by this message and noted wryly that it was not one of the proverbs repeated by Mother in my hearing, not even in reference to others.

'There was nothing spontaneous in their lives. Everything was preplanned. They did themselves out of surprises. The habit of ritual prevailed like smoke. It got in everywhere and tarnished and suffocated everything. Do you remember how solemnly they celebrated each other's birthday? How expensive and exquisitely wrapped presents had to be? And then there was that piece of theatre that had to be enacted for the exchange of them! Do you remember how Lisa changed for dinner up to the day she closed the house and went down to Stroud with Harold? Many of those evenings early on in the war, when you were away at school and Charlotte was in America, she dined alone in all her finery. Lisa regarded my more relaxed attitude to protocol as being designed perversely to shock. It was beyond her imagination to conceive of someone raised within shouting distance of Papa's house in Baden-Baden who could lead life so differently. But I believe in a way it was consoling for her to see me as perverse. It not only highlighted the rightness of her own standards, it gave her something to criticize me for to George. Poor Lisa, she was born without a hint of humour. It was probably that, above all else, which prevented her from seeing through the veils of conformity.

'They worked hard at enjoyment, but Lisa never quite achieved it. It wasn't only George who fell short of her expectations. She never found other people and other standards quite came up to scratch. Take the opera. She'd always heard better in some provincial German opera-house. Take supper after . . . the wine list. The table was invariably too near the kitchens or the entrance. Whenever I tried to offer George and Lisa a night out, I was made to feel it had been an ordeal rather than a pleasure. Theirs was a double act. Once Lisa dealt the *coup de grâce*, your father interred the offending person or situation.'

All this time, while Walter talked, we had been strolling in the olive-clad hills. As we re-entered the square, the dog, who had accompanied us throughout, flopped down in front of one of the little houses. A woman emerged from behind a bead curtain and shouted at the animal, staring at us with unabashed hostility. I saw Walter take this in but he did not remark on the woman. He went on spilling out years of distaste for Mother and Father.

'I once heard George telling you that if ever you did something again – I forget now what – he would call the police to take you away to the reformatory. He uttered his words with devastating effect. He was, after all, a man who knew *par excellence* how to insert a cartridge in the breech. I was almost as stunned as you when he fired. I watched as you started to shake, and saw your poor little face shrink as it turned white. And when he shouted at you to "get out", I could see that you had real difficulty in moving. You were stuck to the spot with fright. Once you had got out, I told George that he was a bully, that bullies were sadists, and he should stick to men his own size. From the corner of my eye I saw his hand jerk, reaching for his horsewhip. But in the event he changed his mind and stomped out of the room without uttering a word. I think he believed that everyone, including a child, achieves most when he feels a knife at his throat.'

I felt myself flush and I recognized a sensation that included anger and hurt, a sort of righteous indignation.

'He used to go on about my posture and how it was "a reflection of your attitude to life". Pompous oaf! And they both told me that my face would be permanently scarred by my scowls. Did I scowl? Do you remember?'

'*Liebchen!*' Walter was smiling. 'You've caught his voice precisely, and after all these years . . . George was used to soldiers, men he could mould into the stiff, unnatural automata of the parade-ground. You know, his hero was George V and he liked to treat you and Charlotte like soldiers perpetually on parade. He was punctilious about dress and deportment, and like the King's eldest son you rebelled. He couldn't stand meeting his Waterloo, as they say, in his little daughter. No, you didn't have bad posture. . . .' And he laughed. He took me in his arms and pushed up my chin so that he could look directly into my face.

'When you were let out of a locked cupboard or ran screaming from a beating, when I traced you to your hide-out in the bushes, at the end of the orchard, you were like a frightened little animal. I would take you in my arms, like this, and comfort you. When your screams subsided and all that remained of your terror were occasional heaving sobs, I would look into your face and see years of intimidation stored in your expression, many more years than you had actually had to endure. I suppose to exonerate themselves Lisa and George called that expression a "scowl".'

'Why did you never push Father up against a wall and beat him to a pulp?' I buried my face in the soft fabric of his shirt. I was weeping.

When, eventually, Walter answered me he sounded oddly weary. 'I always knew that one day I'd have to face that question. I've dreaded it.'

We were lying on the bed in our little room, resting from our long walk into the hills. I propped myself on my elbow to look at Walter. His face looked fearful and tired. He slowly got off the bed and moved to the window.

'I was in an equivocal position. On the one hand I used to fantasize torture for him. On the other I knew that, were I to put a foot wrong, I could be shown the door for all time. I decided that if I could do nothing to prevent their abuse of you, at least I could make you understand that I thought you good and beautiful, that I was your friend, that whatever happened I would always be there for you. Of course there must have been lots of times when I wasn't even in the country when you were having a terrible time of it. . . .' Walter paused. 'I think if I'd been living in England permanently I might have dealt with things very differently. I'd have gathered evidence systematically, gone to the NSPCC or the police or some other authority. . . .' He looked sad, hurt and uncomfortable. 'I can assure you, *Liebchen*, their treatment of you used to make me sick with horror. I had nightmares about it.' Walter put his hands over his face and shook his head. 'On those occasions I found myself a spectator. I watched you, uncomprehending, submitting to the cruelty they imposed on you, knowing that you were going to look in my direction and implore me with your eyes to do something. My heart would thump, and then melt. My first reaction was shock – like yours – but that was quickly followed by a feeling that my heart was breaking because of your bewilderment. And I was furious at being implicated in their brutality. I was astonished that nothing of beauty was damaged in you. Somehow you managed to keep clear of their perversity. I vowed never to betray the trust you put in me. You never blamed me in your eyes for being there.'

'Dearest Walter, I'm glad you did as you did,' I reassured him. I was reminded of how I defended him to Hamilton-Barnes. I slipped off the bed and joined him at the window and we looked together out on to the sea. I was genuinely glad he did as he did. Had he confronted Father or stepped between Father and me, Father would have destroyed or exiled him. There is something unassailable in the weight of the absolute authority required by impotent men.

'Once, following a terrible beating your father gave you at the behest of your mother, I went to Lisa to demand the key to unlock you from your room. I begged Lisa that next time she should do to me what she felt inclined to have done to you, and "have mercy on your young bones". Her only response was to shout at me to get out of the house forthwith. It was six months before she had forgotten the incident fully enough to invite me to dinner again.'

While I lay resting in his arms, I drank regenerative peace from Walter. I thought how a bud might feel opening to the sun in flower. And how a hill forms when the earth rumbles, splits open and casts boiling lava across the land.

Our life together spoke of nothing but love. Every daily action, however mundane, spoke of it. But our physical meeting spoke of the ineffable, there was something immoderate about the joy it showered upon us, and it never crossed my mind that either of us could be like this with another partner. Even now, all these years after his death, I have not felt inclined to make love with anyone else, and on the rare occasions I have conceded, it has proved an almost meaningless experience, little more than a parody of what Walter and I knew.

'There were so many things that made me seethe with anger on your account. What other family forbade their daughter entry into the drawing-room unsupervised? God alone knows what *objet d'art*

Lisa imagined was put at risk by your presence. And on the rare occasions we all drove down to that hotel at Box Hill – do you remember the one, it was where I bought you the china beehive filled with honey? – for Sunday lunch, you were invariably carsick, and smacked for it! And Lisa had a theory that any cold brought into the house was your fault. Never hers, never George's, never Nanny's. All contagion had your name on it. But the much more damaging offence was that they never believed you. Whatever you said, they questioned with contempt. I told them repeatedly that if you were telling the truth – as I believed you were – and they went on refusing to believe you, it was an open invitation to you to start lying. They didn't understand the more subtle implication that it might also turn you into the sort of individual who has no consideration for others. Having instructed a false morality, they could never have taught you a true one. It's a miracle you conserved the ability to distinguish good from evil. Whatever the function of Albrecht Kurtz, it wasn't to give them any psychological insights.'

We were lying on our backs facing the fruitwood cross hanging on the whitewashed wall of our little Spanish room. For a second, I was reminded of the fact that Christianity brought back the notion of human sacrifice to a region that had disposed of such barbarity – or so it thought. As incidents from my own experience returned, I felt reintroduced to an isolation from which I imagined I had long since escaped.

'I felt so lonely, so dispossessed.'

Walter caressed me while he spoke. 'Someone once wrote that "good" families are generally worse than others. It's true. Yours concentrated exclusively on its social standing – what it owned, how it conformed. Neither Lisa nor George ever questioned their rightness. For far too long I rather excused their behaviour, thinking of it as malign foolishness rather than evil. But it was evil, and there was something in me that inhibited me from facing the evil in Lisa, particularly, and addressing it. I suppose it was partly because I had known her for so long and never had any inkling of it before she had you. And then, with the whole of Europe consumed by evil, recognizing the same propensity in someone who might herself so easily have been the victim, was somehow too unpalatable. . . .' Walter had me tightly enclosed in his arms.

'She didn't have to like me. She had to love me. I'm a bit of herself. The trouble is they neither of them liked themselves, really. That was their trouble and they made it mine.'

'I found it unbearable to watch you craving Lisa's affection. But while it was pitiful to watch, it would have been worse if I'd acknowledged to myself that what you craved actually didn't exist. I consoled myself by thinking that it was better that you should cling to the prospect of a loving relationship with your mother than that you should give up on her and it, and see her for what she was, and come to hate her.'

'Better?'

'In the sense that it would do less damage to your emotional life in the long run if you retained some hope in the present that one day she would find and express affection for you. And you really did put yourself out to do all you could to win her over. Between the beatings and the verbal abuse, the threats to withdraw privileges, you complimented her on her appearance, you bought her little presents with your pocket-money, you stroked her arm and buried your face in her furs, you ran errands for her and you repeatedly told her how much you loved her. It brought tears to my eyes to hear you beg "Mummy! Mummy! Do you love me? Do you love me?" But for George you felt nothing but terror. I've seen you wet your knickers at the sound of his key in the front door.'

'Oh God!' And I wept. I wept for years of distress, because then in Walter's arms it was safe to do so. I repeated to Walter the litany of abuse hurled at me by Mother. I rehearsed for him the threats made by Father. 'Why did they do it? Were they mad or something?'

'She did it out of jealousy. He did it out of inadequacy. It had nothing to do with you. You were simply the scapegoat. The present for Lisa was so overshadowed by what might have been – her romantic construct – and, perhaps, by what would be.'

'Why do you imagine she tolerated you and me?'

'There must have been a whole complex of reasons, but one of the unconscious ones, I believe, was that Lisa only felt a sense of her existence in pain. She had something of the masochist in her – and something of the exhibitionist and the sadist. Her jealousy fuelled her fantasy.'

I was crying. Like the waters of a river in spate, it seemed the tears would never stop. Through my sobs I related to Walter how, when I tried to kiss Mother's cheek, she would turn away, my mouth landing on her hair, coarse as a dog's. How when I told her that my friend Phoebe's mother put her on her knee and let her smother her with kisses, read her stories, took her to the zoo, did jigsaws with her, Mother snorted, telling me that I had a nanny for that sort of thing.

'In the whole five and a half years I was stuck up in Northumberland, neither of them ever came up. They hardly ever wrote. Father was alive for two of those years, and some of that time he was in England, on leave. . . . I felt completely abandoned. I loved it when you came. Tell me, how did you manage to get round Miss Langdale? I thought – we all thought – only fathers and brothers of the male species were allowed.'

'I told her I was your uncle. Lisa told me to do so. It absolved her from making the journey – and she certainly didn't want Harold putting in an appearance! I don't think Miss Langdale believed I was your uncle for a moment, but soap, nylons and the occasional steak made up for any inconsistencies she spotted.'

'The girls used to ask me if you were *really* my uncle, and because I couldn't tell a proper lie I told them that you were a friend of my father. I sensed that I shouldn't say "of my mother". . . . Funny how children know these things without knowing quite why. What a seducer you are! Miss Langdale was supposed to hate men.'

'Oh, I don't think she did. I used to write to her and ask for news of you – your progress at work, your health, whether you were making friends. . . . And she wrote back. She told me all I needed to know to ease my anxieties. Your own little letters were delightful but terribly sad. I needed all the reassurances I could get. But equally, I needed to honour your trust. I'd never responded to that of others. I'd let down a lot of people by then.'

I stopped weeping. Walter disengaged himself from me and sat up, his legs dangling over the side of the bed. I noticed how he stared at the cross. He said something about having rejected his father's way of life and despising his brothers for adopting it, and how as a result he had become implicated in their fate.

'It's a terrible burden. I didn't care whether they lived or died, but I never imagined how they would be consumed.'

I had nothing to say to this, but suddenly I was mindful of the absolute necessity for compassion and consideration towards those I did not like. I felt uneasy, because even if I had maintained positive feelings towards Mother as a child, I had certainly aban-

doned them in adulthood. Walter imagined I was vindicated because throughout my childhood I avoided becoming bitter and
continued to value the love I was denied. He was unaware of how
deeply I hated Mother then. I don't think he realized that one can
love and hate at the same time.

A peculiar contrapuntal dirge plays in my head as Walter returns
to bed, lies down beside me and whispers endearments, and I can
hear Mother's litany of insults and complaints.

'*Liebchen*, my beloved. . . . Say you're sorry! Beg my forgiveness!
Let me kiss you again . . . and again . . . I'm deeply ashamed of you.
You'll come to a very sticky end. You are a liar and a cheat. I should
be failing in my duty as a mother if I did not report your insolence
to your father! My beautiful, my dearest love. . . .' Walter is
drawing me to him, and as he fondles a lock of my hair I feel
Mother pulling it, twisting my ear. 'Beloved! Beast! Vermin!
Sweetest child, exquisite lover. . . . Yes, you may have been
naughty from time to time, but it was they who were wicked and
cruel. And throughout their reign of terror you kept yourself pure.
You suffered, you witnessed but did not judge. . . .'

Sticks and stones broke my bones but names will always hurt
me.

It has been said that there is no political regime that can
indelibly scar its victims more than that of an English middle-class
nursery. But being only half English, I had to endure not only the
peculiar mores of the nursery, but those of a foreign parent – and
the calculated cruelty of both my parents. The crabbed experience of my childhood is unendurable to recall. But that is what I
do. I remember that nothing valuable was made available to me.
Music was denied me for being Mother's domain. Great books, for
not being understood by Father, were regarded as the special
province of a section of the community they both envied – and
therefore despised. 'You wouldn't understand a word, Antonia.'
Sport was unsuited to an awkward child whose posture was deplor-
able. 'You'd look a pretty picture on the tennis-court. . . .' And,

anyhow, coaching was an 'extra'. The misery of school was made worse by my having nowhere to run to, no escape, no family in whom to confide its horrors.

Sometimes, today, I read in autobiographies of people who have achieved some success of the care their parents took to introduce them to the wonders of the world and to share in the experiences. I do not know whether to weep or rage. And it is erroneously assumed that the only children who are abused are those from poor families.

Wer nie sein Brot mit Tränen ass, Wer nie die kummervollen Nachte Auf seinem Bette weinend sass, Der kennt euch nicht, irh himmlishcen Machte. Oh Walter, Walter, if only you were alive now to walk with me in this garden and repeat those words to me as once you did. Night after night you come bidden in my dreams, quoting Goethe, your arms filled with *Liebchen* roses. I am intoxicated with expectancy, only to be dashed by grief. Mother always said that one day God would punish me for the shame I brought on the family.

In the canvas bag Madge had packed the *John and Mary* books that tell of happy family life. I did not remember much of the stories, only the atmosphere of sublime happiness I experienced while reading them. There was a world, somewhere, where mothers and fathers who loved one another, loved their children. They lived in cosy houses with small gardens, where clean washing flapped dry on lines slung between the boughs of ancient apple trees. There were unconventional aunts with cropped hair who rode bicycles and organized amateur theatricals. There were dogs and cats of no discernible breed which shared the sofa and the bed. There were expeditions to the Lakes and on narrow boats on the Kennet and Avon Canal. Wet tomato sandwiches and jam puffs in the garden, in which the children's friends shared. There was Snap and Happy Families round the log fire, and toast made on long toasting-forks, and story-telling. All so different from my experience at the house in the avenue. We rarely did anything together as a family, and if and when something was planned, a row would break out and everything would be spoilt, or cancelled.

I thought back to the violent fights my parents used to have with one another.

'Please make up! Please be friends!' I prayed. But not to God: to them. Once I saw Father push an empty tin with a jagged edge into Mother's face. Once I saw her grab him between the legs, and twist. Their raised voices shattered the deathly quiet that shrouded the house. These fights made me feel physically sick and weak at the knees. I was reminded of those feelings only recently – when, walking in the country, I stepped on a dead rabbit seething with maggots.

Mother was never open to criticism. She conveyed to me her conviction that, in the face of a parent, a child was invariably and inevitably wrong. As I grew older, I realized that her self-image was such that she did not dare to admit to the tiniest shortcoming for fear of calling her entire existence in question. A case in point was her handwriting. She had the habit of forming her m's so that they looked like w's. I asked her why she formed these letters upside-down, and held up the piece of paper to show her what I meant. She denied the evidence of our eyes. Years later a friend told me that if her husband were to find her in bed with another man and ask her what on earth she was doing, she would tell him that she was waiting for a bus. 'Always deny,' she explained.

Together with me and my reputation, Mother sacrificed the truth with almost primitive zeal. But it was not to placate the gods, not to bring rain or diminish violence in our little community, merely to enhance her authority, to confer on her emotional and social inadequacy – and on Father's emotional and sexual inadequacy – a sort of ritual. Looking at it coolly, I can see that Mother must have felt herself perilously insecure to have had to depend on the annihilation of her younger daughter to give her confidence. As for Father, his implication in my destruction was particularly tawdry, for he never abused me spontaneously but only on Mother's instructions. Since they did not understand loyalty to one another, but only a very poor substitute lodged in a fear to disagree, neither could be loyal to the truth.

It was natural perhaps that in later years my specialism became human sacrifice. But it is surprising that, despite the natural talent I had for research and evaluation, and my determination that my work should scrupulously conserve the evidence for the sake of future generations, I failed completely to make reasoned sense of my own sacrifice. I had no difficulty in finding excuses for my parents' behaviour, but I never found altogether satisfactory reasons. I have often wondered how they managed to sleep peacefully. What sort of consciences did they have, if any? What moral gloss did they apply to their actions? For there were no extenuating circumstances to account for their brutality: they both came from privileged homes, they were both well loved, neither had been brutalized. That Mother's fragile self-esteem was shored up by demolishing my own, describes rather than explains her behaviour. By placing me in the shadows of continuous disgrace, she placed herself in a sunnier light, but that does nothing to account for why she needed to jostle for position. It was as if some echo from the biblical past reached her: there has to be a bloody deed for there to be salvation.

My soul murder conferred a sort of sanctity on Mother. I believe she felt the need to expunge an impurity she saw manifested in me but identified as belonging to herself. Perhaps it was an impurity she had always sensed as vaguely present but which lay dormant. It was the misalliance she made with Father that provoked it and showed itself in behaviour which was extreme and provided an object – both herself and not herself – upon which to vent her disgust.

Mother's fury, and the power she had over Father to mete out my punishments, raised her to heights she otherwise did not attain. She seemed to grow physically as her self-confidence swelled. Yet, hitting me herself or verbally abusing me was never quite as fulfilling as when she delegated these punishments to Father. By not getting involved personally she not only not avoided the messy side but implicated her husband who, as her initiate, was grateful to be accorded a role in which he gained her favours.

I noticed that after brutal exorcisms, Mother's behaviour towards me softened slightly. She regarded me as less evil than before the chastisement, and thus less dangerous to have about the house.

It has always struck me as odd that a circumstance which had barely affected me had been so decisive for Walter. It was the evening on which he discovered that Mother had excluded me from what promised to be a very dreary dinner party that proved the final straw for him. He never dined at the house again.

In the course of the afternoon of the dinner, Mother rang Walter and asked him to come over in good time because there was a matter she wished to discuss with him that she preferred not to go into on the telephone. She had to come to a decision about the seating arrangement, so that the parlourmaid could distribute the place-cards by a given time. Walter duly turned up early. Mother described the various people she had invited that evening. She would seat her friend Marguerite on her fiancé's right, but who was she to seat on his left? Which of the army wives did Walter imagine would be the least offended? Walter was not acquainted with all the guests and would not have been competent, even had he been willing, to advise Mother. However, he had a way of taking a sounding of her inclinations in advance of her, and gently propelling her in the direction she had unconsciously decided to move. This gift had the result of confirming Mother, assisting her to get her way. In addition, there were the wines to decide upon. This involved a short discussion, a journey down to the cellar that Mother never made herself, the selection of the chosen wine, an adjustment to the list of bottles posted on the cellar door and, in the event of the chosen vintage having been already consumed, a decision as to an alternative.

It was at about six-thirty that Walter emerged from the cellar and bumped into me in the hall, where he learnt that Mother had instructed me to eat my dinner in the maids' sitting-room. He was speechless. I repeated Mother's instruction because I was not sure he had understood, and as I turned to continue upstairs I heard him slam down the bottles he was carrying on the hall table, barge into the drawing-room and start yelling in German. I stopped in my tracks, and within seconds heard Mother start to wail and Walter exit the room shouting *Das genugt!* several times. I ran back down the stairs, but before I could reach him, Walter had left, slamming the front door behind him. Later, I overheard Mother telling Charlotte to get hold of Uncle Harold. 'I need a man to officiate this evening,' she said as tragically as she knew how, 'and see to it that Antonia's not hanging round the stairs or the hall when the guests arrive.'

I was always conscious that Mother's relations with her brother were not of the best. It was not until I went to live with Walter, however, that I discovered just how displeased Mother had been when Harold arrived on her doorstep in the late 1930s. It was not that he presented himself as a liability; he was already something of a financial wizard and would be well able to fend for himself. It was because she would have to integrate him socially, and she might be called upon to account for his unmarried status.

'He wasn't stupid,' Walter allowed, 'but only serious about business and boys. And he was utterly unencumbered by sensitivity.'

I remember Uncle Harold as a rather pathetic character, none the less one I found peculiarly unwholesome and did not wish to have near me. I was outraged as a child that I was expected to submit myself to his kisses – and return them. I was relieved that Father resolutely refused to include Harold when fellow-officers and their wives were invited, occasions upon which Nanny had to bring me into the drawing-room, suitably dressed, for me to say good-evening to the guests. At the time I thought it was because of Uncle Harold's appearance. I imagined that Father, who was so fussy about appearances, found Harold as repellent as I did. He had watery, pale, bulging eyes (he reminded me of a cod), ruddy cheeks and thin, greasy fair hair. But it was his lips that were his worst feature: only loosely connected, it seemed, to his face muscles.

I thought back to the Stroud days, and to Uncle Harold's lips, and how they haunted the few holidays I spent in their company. They had a life of their own, and I dreaded the appearance on the table of the cold soups Mother had prepared in the summer – fruit soups and borscht. (I wondered whether it was the taste of those soups that made me dislike them to this day, or whether it was the image of their journey from the plate to Harold's lips.) I used to try not to watch Harold when he was eating, but somehow I was hynotically drawn to his face. With every spoonful I shuddered as his lips failed him, never quite managing to close round the full complement of liquid he drew into his mouth on a sucking hiss, but flapping fat, loose and uncontrolled, and allowing the carmine fluid to make rivulets down his chin, eventually staining the napkin he wore round his neck.

What was it I cooked when I was first plunged into domestic life with Walter? I had never been encouraged to learn to prepare food. At school cooking was not taught, and at home I had been urged constantly not to 'bother' Cook with my presence in the kitchen. We could not have lived on the diet of fairy cakes and fudge that Barbara had taught me to make when I was about seven. Food must have had mixed associations for me, forced as I was to eat whatever was put on my plate, however little to my taste, and often I was exiled to my room to eat bread and milk alone. On the rare occasions when the whole family assembled for a meal in the dining-room, the tense atmosphere took away my appetite.

'We do not discuss politics, religion or personal matters at table,'
Mother reminded me after the war. 'Personal matters' was
Mother's euphemism for sex. We did, however, discuss my table
manners both before and after the war. They always proved a
disappointment to Mother. 'Where on earth did I get you from?' she
asked in despair. 'Didn't Nanny insist on better than this in the
nursery?' I must 'sit up straight', remove my elbows from the table,
cease to fidget, wait to be passed what I require, stop pushing my
food round my plate, say 'thank you' and 'please may I have'. All
these instructions were issued irrespective of who was sharing a
meal with us. Eating became quite a problem for me – that is to say,
eating in the company of others.

Walter and I agreed on simply prepared food. I imagine that
Walter's decision was arrived at largely on account of cost, even if
he were mindful both of my lack of experience at the kitchen
stove and my trials at table. Food in Britain, at the time, was not
generally plentiful, and lacked variety. Some items were still
rationed. But that was not the reason why, for months, I served a
hearty English breakfast three times a day. Eventually and with tact
Walter weaned us from this diet by giving me a copy of *Clarisse or
The Old Cook*, a discursive book, as much to read as to follow, with
liberal asides on poets and novelists – French, of course – whose
characters enjoyed food and later, on publication, Elizabeth
David's *Italian Food*. It was then that I stopped dreaming about
Emma Bovary's wedding breakfast, Theodore de Banville's sandwiches, and under what victuals Madame de Mortsauf's elegant
table groaned, and went from beef, lamb and eggs *à la* Richelieu, *à
la* Milton, *à la chasseur*, to the more sunny side of food. We lived on
pasta and pizza, I think. Indeed, if I am right, we strove for
simplicity, put off lavish food by recalling the spreads that Mother
laid on for her guests, reflecting her insensitivity to the times.

Mother had retained her Stroud contacts, and the dishes that
Cook prepared from the ingredients supplied by the farmers who
had become Mother's closest associates during the war never
failed to arouse from her acquaintances the enthusiastic response
she craved. Walter and I wondered what the officers and their
wives – dealt far weaker hands by their suppliers – said behind
Mother's back after she had once again trumped their efforts.

The black market in Britain during the war had not been run
exclusively by and for the Jewish population, as was implied by

much of the press. But the facts did nothing to alter people's perceptions, the most popular being that Jews were eating better than non-Jews, and since the war was being waged for the sole benefit of the Jews . . . et cetera et cetera. A number of Jewish men and women were caught *in flagrante* and imprisoned *pour faire un exemple*.

'I don't pay a penny over the odds,' Mother objected, when I pointed out to her that she had not given coupons for anything on the table at Stroud. 'If you have objections, just don't eat,' she advised me, adding that I did not understand how things were conducted in the country and, in any case, it was none of my business. Despite the awful muck we were served at school, I did not want to benefit from the spoils exacted by Mother. I remember being relieved that she never allowed me to invite a friend to Stroud.

I repacked the canvas bag, carefully placing Mr Bear on top of the books and the walnut box and zipping the bag closed only as far as his nose. I then walked across the lawn in the direction of the porch and Harold's garden furniture. It struck me that it was as overblown as his lips, and the covers as tasteless as the suits he had made for himself. I had no idea if Harold had a heart of gold. Walter had vouched for his insensitivity, and what I saw and heard of him I found so off-putting as to preclude all such considerations. Yet he had no doubt had a tough time of it. I do not imagine he fulfilled himself. Probably that was what spurred him on to make money. Where was he now that his only sister was dying? I had forgotten to ask Charlotte and she had not told me.

It was dawn. Mother must be dead by now. I was ready for the formal letters of condolence. I dreaded them. I did not care for letters.

It was shortly after Walter and I returned from Spain that Walter found the little bundle of letters from Mother and Father that I had kept.

'What in the world possesses you to hang on to these? It isn't healthy!' Walter added that he would be consigning them to the fire. Before doing so, he selected a couple to read out loud. First, the one Mother sent from Stroud, informing me that the roses had arrived dead and that it was she who paid the postage. Then one from Father, complaining how thoughtless I was to ask him to visit me at school: 'Haven't you heard there's a war on!' This was followed by a closely written page about the daughter of a fellow-officer 'as clever as she's obedient; as pretty as she's wise'.

'Were there a god, and were I to pray to him, I would ask that he take vengeance on your parents. In the case of George it would involve a long sojourn in hell right away, and in the case of Lisa that same treatment to look forward to all in good time. But, of course, there is no god. . . .'

I had rarely seen Walter so discomposed.

Years after Walter died, I went back to work for the anti-fascist group of which I had been a member during my adolescence. As a result of articles and letters in the press on the subject of racism, I attracted hate mail. The writers of this abuse would have been disappointed to learn that, having received so much from my parents, I never read through theirs. I would open the invariably misspelt, unpunctuated, unstamped envelopes, take in the first sentence, and quickly replace the letter in its envelope. Hate mail was dealt with by a solicitor instructed by our group to liaise with the police. But merely handling written abuse had an immediate physical effect on me: my throat would contract, my stomach knot and my blood run cold.

When I was a child, I knew that everything that gave pleasure originated with Walter. But when I grew up and lived with him, his unstinting and imaginative generosity embarrassed me. I found it uncomfortable to accept all he insisted I deserved. I had been programmed to believe that, if ever I deserved anything at all, it would be something cheap or second-hand. And so I automatically went to quite elaborate pains to avoid having to accept lavish presents from Walter.

My parents were not naturally generous. But it was because of their lack of affection that they were stingy with presents for me. They could be relied upon to withhold from me even the little things I longed for on the grounds of my insolence, my thought-lessness and my lack of achievement, whichever was the current preferred excuse. Birthdays and Christmases were a perennial torture. I could never be sure whether I stood a chance of getting the thing for which I longed, or whether I would be fobbed off with a pad of Basildon Bond and the exhortation to behave better in future.

Mother had me kitted out in Charlotte's cast-offs. These were of excellent quality (far better, I suppose, than she would have bought new for me) and always reached me in impeccable condition. Charlotte wore her clothes only until she tired of them. No one, seeing me in these garments, would have dreamt they were not new, so no one questioned Mother's practice. As soon as Charlotte had discarded a coat or dress, Nanny would wash and iron it, or have it dry-cleaned, slip lavender bags between the folds, wrap it in tissue-paper and pack it in a huge Debenham and Freebody box decorated with peacocks. I never enjoyed wearing these garments but rarely found the courage to ask Mother for anything new, knowing she would say that because the cupboard in my tiny bedroom was so small, there was no space in which to hang new things. By the time I was five I had rumbled that excuse, but I knew it was useless to remonstrate.

When I went to live with Walter, I found it difficult to cope with his passionate interest in my clothes and almost impossible to welcome his insistence that he accompany me when I bought anything for myself. Mary Quant's 'Bazaar' was fashionable at the time, and I recollected our expeditions to the King's Road with toe-curling unease. Walter would stand reflectively by the rails, then pick out half a dozen dresses and suits for me to try on. While I changed into his choices, he searched for more. When I emerged from the dressing-room, he watched with anxious pleasure. Did I like it? 'You look wonderful, *Liebchen*! The grey stripes suit you perfectly. The pink goes so well with your own colouring. . . . White is gloriously impractical – you must have it. You could wear your silver chains with any of them. . . .'

Walter had given me three antique silver chains, designed to be worn as a belt but which he liked me to wear as a necklace. The chains were snakelike, joined head and tail with large beaten-silver beads. I still have them somewhere, but I should prefer not to come across them. And he would want to pay for whatever I chose. I couldn't bear it. I knew how strapped for cash he was, how he needed to put every penny he made into purchasing further books and manuscripts – and anyhow, my allowance (my legacy from Granny Sinclair) was quite adequate for my needs.

Without taking in details, I had walked right round the perimeter of the orchard and up and down between the rows of fruit trees before I found myself in the rose garden, a sort of parterre with box hedges defining the beds. There had been no place either in the orchard or in this part of the garden for the clamour of colour at the expense of design. How Father must have loved both places! And then I heard a noise in the shrubbery and I was filled with apprehension, pitched back to the night Mother shut me out of the house.

When I was not being physically and verbally battered, I was largely ignored. To make it clear that I was neither needed nor wanted, Mother would treat me as if I were invisible. If I asked her a question, she would not reply. If I ran to show her something – a flower, a pebble – she turned away. Eventually, before banishing me to boarding-school, she hit on the idea of shutting me out of the house. I could not recall the number of times she operated this punishment; the terror of the experiences melded themselves together and left me with the memory of a single occasion.

Father is away. The house seems to have been abandoned. Cook and the parlourmaid are out. I don't know where Mother is. I think she is in the drawing-room. I am playing upstairs. I hear doors slam and Mother screaming. Next, she is dragging me down three flights of stairs by my wrists.

I am dressed in a light summer frock. It is dusk; low shadows are making sinister patterns on the lawn. Mother is still shouting. She pushes me through the french windows on to the porch, where I stand fixedly, holding on to the door-handle, which she locks from the inside. Looking into the drawing-room, I see Mother has turned out the lights and closed the door behind her. Surely she will come back, will fetch me soon. She will let me in again when she is no longer in a temper. 'Mother! Mother!' But I know she cannot hear me. Nothing of the outside can be heard in the house when the windows are shut. I am cold. I am hungry. I don't have my cardigan and I haven't had supper. There is nothing on the porch to sit on and it is getting very dark. I want to go to the lavatory.

I take a deep breath and without looking to right or left I run into the summer-house. I have avoided the ghosts. The ground-sheet and picnic rug are kept here, under the flower and fruit baskets. I lay the groundsheet on the floorboards, wrap myself in the picnic rug and lie down. But I can hear footsteps. Someone is coming! Someone is coming to steal me. It must be the gypsies: 'My Mother said, I never should, play with the gypsies in the wood. . . .' Gypsies abduct rich little girls and return them to their families only when they are paid lots of money. Mother wouldn't pay anything for me. I start to cry.

Why did I so fear abduction? Like other abused children, I did not regard myself as victimized. There was obviously something wrong with me to make my parents hate me so. I preferred to be sentenced to life with them at home than with anyone else anywhere else.

I looked down at my jeans. I had prepared myself for this visit far more suitably than Mother prepared me for nights shut out of the house.

It was starting to rain again. I loved the rain and was grateful for it: it reminded me always of the walk Walter and I took under the nave of *marroniers* along the River Ouanne. Like cognac cupped in warm hands, the earth exudes its special aroma at the touch of rain. Walter and I were in Burgundy. Walter had his arm round my shoulder as we strolled under overhanging branches of sweet chestnut trees. The river flowed quietly and gently at one side of the lane, while on the other we could just make out the turrets of an ancient château. It had been a peak experience for both of us. Seated outside Colette's house in St-Sauveur-en-Puisaye, we spoke of the relationship she had had with her beloved and unusual mother. What would my life have been had I had a Sido?

I walked across the lawn and round the house. All the lights were now extinguished. Oh, Mother, if only you hadn't rejected me. I was so eager to love you and respect you, to accept you as you were, if only you had found it in your heart to love me and show me some affection. As it transpired, heartless and cruel you left me no alternative but to hate you with all my heart and with all my might.

Walter had been wrong about my anger and bitterness. It was intact, waiting to explode when he was no longer there to be disappointed in me.

Resolution

The weak have one weapon: the errors of those who
think they are strong.

Georges Bidault

I SUFFERED MORTAL GRIEF WHEN WALTER DIED. THE WHOLE
purpose of my life had been embodied in him. We were accustomed to one another. We were grateful to one another. We
shared in all our experiences of joy, grief, frustration and ecstasy.
Our intimacy was repeatedly rewarded by a seizure of unexpected
passion, a bonus, which served to remind us that every self has
unexplored areas which remain to be discovered. At first it was the
physical symptoms of indifference and lassitude, leading to terror
and panic, that overwhelmed me, making it impossible for me to
think consistently; just as soon as I determined to consider something seriously, I grew weary. All I could think of was that Walter
was dead. That was all that was real. It was inescapable. The
emptiness held no expectations. It was not stimulating, merely
alarming. Added to which, Walter had fuelled and stoked a passion
in me I had not known I had. His death did not quench it. I was left
in a permanent state of unfulfilment that only he could satisfy.

I do not remember when it was or how it was that I faced the
second reality. Excruciating though his absence was, it was not
merely that which made it impossible for me to speak to others, or
apply myself to my work. Once again I was registering the tremors
of my childhood, suffering the accumulation of ruptures that had
constituted my life.

Walter's death, I told myself, had to be the penultimate rupture.
In the event, however, not only did I lack the energy, I lacked the
courage to effect my own.

I did not say goodbye to him. I could not have borne to see him
mangled and ugly in his suffering. I let the undertakers do all that

131

was required. I did not even go to the crematorium when they consigned him to the flames he had so astutely escaped in the thirties. And when, eventually, I had the courage to seek out his memorial and garland it with flowers from our garden, I could not find his name. I was so confused – tired, tearful – I just gave up and came away. I threw the flowers down on a pile – a sort of generalized memorial. I believed he would return, just walk in one day and sit down at his desk as if he had been on a buying trip and taken a little longer than usual. I could not think of him as dead; that would have been to render him irretrievable.

To say I 'closed' the shop is too active a description of what took place. I simply left the 'Closed' sign turned towards the street, as Walter had finally flicked it. And I left the books and periodicals ranged and stacked where he had put them, and his desk as he had left it. The paraffin stove, I believe, was half filled, the matches lying on the floor beside it. I suppose I felt – because I so fervently hoped for it – that one day Walter would be back to resume work, setting the shop and his desk in motion again. The impossible is not so fantastical when the inevitable is unbearable. The one positive action I took was to lock the door at the bottom of the stairs that led from the flat to the front door, and the door to the shop. This door, the shop door, I did not open for two years. But I left Walter's stick resting against it.

'We looked; we loved and therewith instantaneously, Death became terrible to you and me.' I remember looking at Walter and repeating those lines in my head before I had the abortion. And I remember the circumstances. All sorts of dusty recollections lie in the fissure of memory.

We were having a picnic by the side of the Grand Union Canal. A slick of slime was passing up and down on the water in the breeze; up as far as a rotting barge, down back to the willows, whose branches flicked the surface of the water. There was perfect quiet. Our peace was shattered suddenly by raucous guffawing. A group of Teddy boys had occupied the bridge fifty yards upstream. They had debagged a frail youth, clearly not one of their number, and flung him over the parapet, where he hung over the water. Vulnerable. Humiliated. In fear for his life.

What I foretold all those years ago, experienced in a sudden sense of emptiness in my stomach and an ice-cold patch on my neck, was a poor intimation of the absolute joylessness and *taedium vitae* that were to follow. For Walter and I were essential to one another.

As I think back today, it seems to me that my whole life prior to Walter's death had been a preparation for it. On the one hand loss had been my most constant and deep emotion. On the other, Walter, with whom I had shared psychic space, the time-space between our inner being and the interstices of living, had been my most precious companion. No matter how assiduously one prepares, however, even if unconsciously, it is in vain. Would it have been less painful if I had nursed him through a long illness, or had some short forewarning that would have provided time to tell him of my love and gratitude and my enduring memory? Do all those left behind after an accident suffer as I suffered? Losing the single human being who had given me a sense of my worth, for whom I had been a love-object from babyhood, left me without a touch-stone. Walter had been the measure of all men. He had satisfied me in every particular. He was interesting, informed, funny, beautiful, touching, generous . . . I could go on. But it was not the loss of these qualities that came to mind in those early years of grief: I was consumed by loss itself. All loss accumulated in his death, and my whole being seized up in response to emotional amputation.

Why was it that my early biography had not prepared me? I was experienced in division, dismemberment and separation. I had been part of the toll taken by erosion and disintegration that had led to the decay of my family. I had suffered mortification through misprision. Now I was learning about emptiness, extinction and non-existence – not only Walter's but my own. In the wake of his death I was drawn into nothingness.

'There's nothing to be afraid of, *Liebchen.*'

I was afraid now, gravely so.

Memory is a space for repetition. It is infinitely flexible. I came to resent the capacity of my own to return me, in a split second, the sensation of experiences with Walter that had taken hours to live through. Memory of details gave way to impressions; the very taste, the very smell. These stabs punctured my being as I groped in Stygian darkness. My misery fortified itself on the most in-substantial nourishment. I did not dare, by exulting in past pleasure, to try to reconstitute whole experiences.

Not only did I feel no need to discuss Walter with anyone, I cannot imagine I would have been capable of doing so. Yes, I confirmed over the telephone to Barbara, we had lived together for ten years. But that was all I told her. Yes, ten years, I confirmed to Mrs Anderson, the first person I visited when I found the energy and courage to leave the flat some thirty months following Walter's death. I did wonder at the time whether Barbara or Mrs Anderson read into my reluctance to speak about Walter some embarrassment or shame, or whether they guessed that for me our relationship had been too sound for an autopsy. I never discussed Walter with anyone when he was alive. And if I did feel something approximating to shame, it had nothing to do with Walter and me. It was that, in some peculiar way, I did not feel entitled to my grief. Why should that have been? Perhaps because I had never felt entirely deserving of his love. Instead of grief being a consolation, it started by being an aggressor and transformed itself into a guilty secret. Shut up in the flat, I kept myself safe from further opportunities, from being let down or rejected, or suffering further loss. Once I emerged, I felt I should feel and act as if nothing untoward had happened.

I had perfected the habit of concealing what I felt when I was a child. I did not understand that, with Walter's death, if I had mediated my feeling of loss through words I might have dissipated its essence and robbed it – together with all loss – of its absolute hold over me. Later, when I tried this in psychotherapy, I succeeded only in understanding the theory. It was too late for the old dog to learn new tricks.

I do not know whether I had a breakdown. It did not seem to me that I contained the constituent parts to shatter. I felt myself a single experience of reduction, expressed in inanition. I found it all but impossible to rise out of bed. Had I not had the three little shops selling essentials just over the road, I do not imagine I should have survived. What drew me eventually to seek professional help was the need for unthreatening conversation without social obligation. I remember how I used to try to think what it meant to be in love – and try to recapture something of that feeling – and how I came to realize that, filled as I was with absolute separateness and isolation, I had made it impossible to imagine or re-create the one experience that had overcome both.

Perhaps my grief was exacerbated by something Walter and I shared. This particular element had not seemed self-evident when he was alive but, on reflection, I am sure that he and I partook in the central loneliness of not belonging. The spores of prejudice had rendered us allergic to many of the same situations, and sensitive to the value of others. Alone, without Walter, I found myself defenceless.

Walter believed in the efficacy of good acts. He would insist that by performing a good act we each have an opportunity to make the world a better place, a more human place, for a good act is a human act. Deliberate cruelty is peculiar to the human species. He said it was because I had never fought back, in hatred, that I had avoided sullying myself. But I had; it was only in his company that my hate-filled thoughts did not predominate. Somehow, without Walter, I had no standards to maintain. It was he who set the standards to which I aspired. People may imagine that, as a monument to a partner's love, the mourner is inviolable. That is a false, romantic notion.

Walter had had his sadnesses and his guilt. Whereas both burnt out in my company and softened into ash, mine never did; while he lived he was able to dampen the flames but never to quench them. The memory of my parents' contempt and brutality intruded on the moment, and does so to this day, bringing with it depression, a black beast that clings to my back, arms outstretched, enveloping me in its suffocating embrace.

'There's nothing to be afraid of, *Liebchen*.'

Nothing! This is the awesome madness that follows upon loss and never relinquishes its control. Nothing! That which is only living can only die.

The black cloud carried the sun away. I could find no hope in my hopeless situation. Walter had been my hope. Walter was dead. Total despair defined itself in total lack of courage. I was desolate; I rotted. My store of energy was depleted, I was worthless without my lover.

I courted neglect; but not in so far as my person was concerned. The rigorous upbringing I had had in the avenue and at St Gudula's told in my persistent attention to hygiene. I washed and I bathed. The inertia that overtook me was not impervious to these habits of a lifetime and I obsessively overhauled them. For example, I did not permit myself a visit to the lavatory unless, following upon that function and the washing of my hands, I undertook some other cleansing: my teeth in the morning, my feet in the afternoon. At night I bathed, washed my hair, shaved my legs, cleaned my neck with eau-de-Cologne. So regularly, so slavishly did I perform my rituals that to have avoided any portion of any one of them would have risked my being thrown into an intolerable state of anxiety. Hence I kept my body clean and my psyche in a permanent state of brinkmanship.

Elsewhere I was more successful with neglect. I gave up use of the vacuum cleaner, dusters and cleaning materials. I had heard that, if one did not clean a room for a year, one no longer noticed dust. At first I was uneasy about the accumulation of rubbish. I was not used to scruffiness and hated it. But I was too profoundly apathetic to bestir myself. This was no usual fatigue, the healthy sort that follows on physical exercise, or a week at work. It was something different. I would sit weeping, wishing things were other than they were, but incapable of effecting a remedy. I did little washing-up. I kept a single mug and plate and some cutlery in the sink in water, and washed what I needed when I needed it. I rarely cooked. Sometimes I heated something from a tin or packet, but mostly I ate bread and biscuits and whatever fruit the little corner shop had in stock – overripe bananas and juiceless oranges, if my memory serves me correctly.

The patch of garden that had seemed to us a paradise when Walter was alive became overgrown. Only the *Liebchen* rose-bush flowered valiantly, despite the weeds that tried to strangle it. Looking out of the kitchen window, I saw nothing but an oblong tangle of nettles and buddleia imprisoned between sooty brick walls. And so I avoided the kitchen and lay in bed, or sat in one corner of the sofa in the sitting-room until I had created a hollow that eventually necessitated having the whole sofa resprung. There were days on which I found it impossible to move at all. I would intend to get up, but the message failed to inform my legs. I would panic and weep, knowing there was something very wrong that I was powerless to do anything about, and that I would simply have to wait until the paralysis gave way. I could not understand why I sweated copiously, found myself breathless and sighing, wept unexpectedly and uncontrollably. I knew I was horribly lonely and isolated; I felt it unbearable, yet was incapable of taking any step to haul myself back into the world.

When I did manage to gather the strength and courage to get as far as the little shop for bread and milk and so on, I felt the eyes of passers-by burning into my back, summing me up, and laughing. I felt disgraced. To keep myself going, I would walk in step with the beating of my pulse, an inexorable thud that sounded my doom. My solitary state enveloped me in some visible mantle that made the strangers in the street stare and keep their distance. I wondered: was I speaking my sorrow out loud? Was it this that made them stop in their tracks and take note before moving on? I was oddly thin. My clothes hung off me as if they were cast-offs from a healthier, better-fed woman. My hair was now long, gathered in an elastic band, and my feet were swollen, so I wore slippers in the street. But I could not say 'Good-morning'. 'Good-morning' stuck in my throat. Nor could I meet people's gaze, for people were the object of my fear: they would ridicule me, let me down or reject me altogether. They could invade me and take me over. Colonize me. This was how I was going to be for ever. The word 'eternity' haunted me.

Eternity was an abstraction that had made my head spin and ache in good times. Now I felt that I might be sent mad being imprisoned, with the word 'eternity' my only companion, in a place where the dead and the unborn reside. The more I sought to replace eternity with another word, the more obstinately it attached itself to my mind. I was a rock, washed over by grief, to which a million molluscs of the genus *eterne* were fastened.

I was eventually awakened by a dream. I dreamt dark. The space in my head was saturated with starless, moonless, impenetrable dark. And then a word, the meaning of which was unfamiliar to me, started to emerge at the corners of the dark: 'olitory'. The word was light; little by little it shrank the corners of the dark so that slowly, gradually, blue emerged and dissolved the dark. I found myself composing a garden: an evocation of paradise.

I was standing at the centre of a square of ground between weathered brick walls. I knew that I must divide the square into four equal parts and lay little sandy paths between and, where they crossed, that I must plant an everlasting, flowering tree and round it place a circular iron bench. I set to. In each of the quarters of land I planted medicinal herbs, scented flowers and bushes which I contained in low box hedges. My work did not fatigue me; I was suffused with satisfaction. I sat down on the iron bench and breathed in fragrant peace and safety.

I woke from this dream consoled. I thought I understood its meaning, and with cosmological order re-established in my unconscious it seemed to me that my conscious mind might be going to experience easier times.

Through the walls of my bedroom I heard the sound of Callas singing 'Remember Me'. I sat up in bed and heard a piercing yell. Seconds later I realized that the anguished yell came from my own throat. Whilst realizing that I was screaming, I did not stop but shrieked on, loud and long. Yet it was not the song that was sending me berserk. It was the sheer sensuousness of the human voice giving expression to something precise that reminded me of the softness of Walter's skin, the expression of desire in his eyes, the faint accent that lent his English its unforgettable voluptuousness, the weight of his body over my own, the thrill as he penetrated me. . . .

Of course I shall remember . . . always. That's the trouble: I have no alternative. Or do I? Do I want to remember for all time? Would I rather not be without the everlasting, searing pain?

It was about three years after Walter's death that I received a letter through the post addressed to 'The Occupier'. I was not immediately suspicious of it, since I had had a number of similarly addressed letters from property speculators, gauging that Camden Town was ripe for development. Yet it was only because this particular letter was stamped that I opened it. Normally, I threw away unsolicited mail unopened.

The letter came from solicitors in the City – Messrs Baum, Hodges and Kirkpatrick. Mr Hodges wrote asking 'The Occupier' to be so good as to telephone his secretary to make an appointment to come along and see him, 'at a time and on a day convenient to us both'. The matter was 'confidential'.

I thought at first that perhaps a property company – interested in purchasing possibly the whole street for development – was attempting a more subtle approach than usual, in an effort to achieve greater success with the owner-occupiers than had, to date, been the case. Most of our street belonged to a company that let their properties. Just half a dozen were lived in by the freeholders. Although I did not have the least desire to move, for practical as well as sentimental reasons, Mr Hodges's letter made me realize that I had no idea where Walter had put the lease for safekeeping. Perhaps with Messrs Baum, Hodges and Kirkpatrick? It was when we were in Spain that Walter had told me that, in the event of his death, I would find the envelope containing his will in the locked drawer of his desk. What I found was a piece of typed paper, witnessed by two strangers, stating that everything of his should go to Antonia Sinclair. It never occurred to me that the shop and flat were not his, or that he did not intend me to go on living there and do with the premises whatever I wanted. I knew he had no savings; I knew that he depended upon his sales for new stock. A few outstanding bills arrived after his death and these I paid out of my own money. I had been so undermined, so incapacitated by his abandonment of me, practical considerations hardly touched me. I suppose that, had I been insolvent, I might have been obliged to look into Walter's affairs.

I set off for the solicitors in the morning, even though my appointment with Mr Hodges was for the afternoon. I had not been in the City since Walter's death and I decided to revisit some of the Wren and Hawksmoor churches that he and I had got to know together. It was a stupid thing to have attempted. I found myself quite unable to appreciate architecture and, in particular, the sound of an organist practising, for the stabs of pain that lacerated me. It seemed to me that for all time everything in its own right beautiful and significant would be nothing but torture to me.

I arrived at Baum, Hodges and Kirkpatrick, close by the Monument, in something of a daze. The secretary, Miss Paterson, introduced herself and directed me to a Rexine-covered chair beside a rickety table on which were old copies of *Country Life* and *Horse and Hound*. I remember thinking that Miss Paterson had probably been with the firm since she left school, some time in the nineteenth century, and had not felt it to be part of her job to flick a duster. My impatience with the selection of magazines, the frayed and dusty green lino, and the person of Miss Paterson, was a reflection of the way in which I distracted and defended myself against the pain I was feeling.

Mr Hodges made me think of Mr Pickwick and I was momentarily reassured. His old-fashioned manners, his mutton chops and florid complexion were perfectly in keeping with the Dickensian atmosphere of his offices. Somewhere to the right or left of his office, no doubt, a thin scribe was writing out wills with a quill pen.

The comforting literary illusion quickly faded once I had settled into a capacious armchair. Was I the late Mr Huberman's . . . er . . . friend? Had I shared the accommodation with him? Was I aware that the shop and flat above did not belong to him?

'I'm afraid, dear lady, I have the distasteful obligation to convey to you that you are not entitled to be living there! I am going to have to ask for your assurance that you will vacate the premises within three months. My client has had an offer for the building that she cannot refuse.'

In passing, Mr Hodges referred to his client as Mrs Helen Schoenfeld, who had set up Mr Huberman in his book business when he was demobilized.

'They had been very close, you understand. . . . I understand there was some . . . er . . . disagreement between them and my client went to America five years ago. She was very shocked to learn of Mr Huberman's death on her return.'

I left Mr Hodges's office more stunned than when I had entered it. A single word echoed round my head: Betrayed! Betrayed by Walter! It was unthinkable. Yet, was it? And what did I mean by betrayal?

I walked home and thought back. During our years together I had been studying and working, and Walter had been working. We had been apart, sometimes for as much as five days on end when he was in the north of the country. There had been plenty of time for him to lead a double life. And it came back to me that there had been the odd occasion when Walter had closed the door to take a telephone call and had seemed to conceal a letter. I remembered: I had felt jealous. Once, Mother had related the story of a man who had had two families in two adjacent provincial towns. It was not until his death that his wives discovered each other's existence. Who was this Mrs Helen Schoenfeld, this 'very close friend' who was about to make me homeless? How could Walter have died without making provision for me?

As I walked I wept.

Should I contact Mrs Schoenfeld? If I wrote to her care of Mr Hodges, he would no doubt forward my letter. But did I really want to learn the details of Walter's relationship with this woman? What had they rowed about? Had it been about me? Had she issued an ultimatum, saying that unless he left me she would sever relations with him? Was she an 'old' friend both in age and time? Her name suggested she might be a refugee, like Walter, or married to one. Perhaps they shared a history. Was Mr Schoenfeld dead or alive when Walter knew her? Dead, I imagined. That must have been how she came by the money to set Walter up in business. Were they lovers? The thought twisted my gut.

A whited sepulchre!

In the confusion of my feelings, there arose a certain bloody-mindedness. I was faced with a mere practical problem and I was going to solve it to my satisfaction: I was not going to move. Whatever Walter and Mrs Schoenfeld's relationship, his and mine had taken place on these premises, and no one was going to evict me from them.

I consulted a solicitor who had acted once or twice for Mother. It was a peculiar choice to have made. It was as if I had needed to cling to the hull of my own wreck. Through him I discovered that for all his seeming respectability and old-worldliness, Mr Hodges's sole concern was for the interests of his client, regardless of my rights under the law. It was indeed true that the freehold belonged to Mrs Schoenfeld but I was certainly not obliged to vacate the place.

I bought it. I might have remained as a statutory tenant but I chose what seemed to me the greater security. Security was a relative matter, which I had discovered along the way. Bricks and mortar were likely to be more reliable than flesh and bones, I decided ruefully.

Some few months before this event, I noticed that I was emerging from what had seemed an intractable stasis. I started to be able to follow my thought from proposition to elaboration and on to some conclusion. I considered returning to work: that would deflect me from my pain. The ritual of sacrifice . . . still a topic of interest . . . I might write up my findings. . . .

A sort of intellectual suppleness came back to me and, as I exercised, became increasingly flexible. My imagination was re-kindled. Then came Mr Hodges's bombshell. I had already accepted an invitation, via my contacts with biblical scholars in Israel, where a group had formed itself for the purpose of comparing Christian and Jewish attitudes to ritual sacrifice, to travel to West Africa and study piacular sacrifice. It was during this sabbatical, in the company of Professors Yehuda and Lodge, that I found myself almost utterly inhibited from making contact with people, whether colleagues, acquaintances or strangers. I had nothing to say over and above communicating my immediate findings. And then even that became difficult. I blushed and stuttered, as if embarrassed. I understood why: I felt their expectation that I should reveal myself and I feared deeply to do so. Our subject, the one that had brought us out here, was too near to my problem.

I returned to London earlier than I had planned. I shopped around for a psychiatrist. A description of the distinguished and less distinguished might be edifying but it is not something I wish at present to record. However, I took care not to settle on one for whom my 'transference' was imperative and chose an elderly German, from Baden-Baden, to whom I went just once a week. As I came to understand the full extent of the damage done to me by Mother and Father, far from becoming less angry, I became more so. Despite the intimacy I developed with this therapist, I did not confide Walter's betrayal, if that is what it was. I tried to believe that, once Walter could no longer make use of Mother, he had simply found another woman to take that role in his life. We all have faults. Walter was sentimental; the obverse side of that particular coin is a sort of steely quality that can lead to making use of people. So I decided to tidy Mrs Schoenfeld out of my mind.

I was seeking therapy at this time because my professional life was at risk. I had become so nervous about making judgements for fear of being wrong that my research was inconclusive. I preferred not to present any argument rather than risk revealing flaws in my thought processes. And in conversation, the fact that my stuttered considerations were punctuated by suggestions of wild spontaneity that tended to lead to correct conclusions did nothing to impress my colleagues. Indeed, the very fact of my intuition challenged their authority and I shut up, terrified that they might react as Father had.

However, by the time I visited Mother on her deathbed, I had improved and was functioning. My research was completed and I had tenure at the college at which I taught. I had redecorated the flat, made the shop into my study and re-established the garden. At last I no longer sat at home conjugating the verb *s'ennuyer*.

'Those who do not remember the past are condemned to relive it.' Until that afternoon when, consumed by indifference, as I thought, I entered the jaws of hell to bid a last adieu to Mother, I had consigned the distant past to the past. But what I had not realized was that, far from dominating it, I had been continuously,

if unconsciously, possessed by it. I imagined that all I had had to
overcome was the loss of Walter, muddied by a vague unease that
he too might have betrayed me. Dr Steiner encouraged me to
bring to our sessions only those matters I wished to discuss. It was
his professional belief that we should deal only with the present. In
the present, I insisted that it was the loss of Walter that overshadowed my existence. But that afternoon and evening, in the
space of no more than six or seven hours under the family roof, I
was borne back into the deep past to collect its burden and bear it
in perpetuity. Walter's death had been the fuse that ignited the
ineluctable charge. Since when 'We two have kept house, the
Past and I', and I have never had any real hope for the future.

I suspect that the importance Mother attached to her Jewishness dated from the moment she married a non-Jew in church. I
believe she must have felt some atavistic guilt and that it was this
that motivated her subsequently to join a synagogue in London.
She chose the one at which the most assimilated British Jews
worshipped in the English language. It was a cold institution. The
congregation tended to forge more links with church and chapel
than with other Jewish sects, and regarded orthodoxy as both
archaic and socially inferior. And anything mystical was too
anarchic for members of the Society of Ethical Monotheists. At
their services there was no mystery, no true religious feeling, but
mere prohibitions initiated by an unseen authority and passed on to
the well-heeled by a man in a well-cut suit. I was dragged along to
services on many of the most holy days in the Jewish calendar and I
was struck how much more comfortable Mother obviously felt
among these ruthlessly genteel English Jews than with Father's
military colleagues. I could not have been more than nine at the
time, for I stopped attending synagogue at the outbreak of the
war. I remember how Mother insisted that I keep my white gloves
on throughout the service and my mouth tight shut when we
trooped out at the end. And I remember that Charlotte knew what
was expected of her without being told. She always did what
Mother deemed 'appropriate', and was pushed forward to be introduced to the various members of the congregation, who in turn
were encouraged by Mother to ignore me. Charlotte not only
attended synagogue with Mother but – and I am sure this was not

communicated to Mother's Jewish friends – church with Father. Although this arrangement did not strike me as odd when I was a child, as an adult I realized that such divided loyalty probably accounted for a great deal.

I believe that Mother's strict adherence to the letter of the moral law was especially tight for its being imparted without ritualistic overtones: there was little in Ethical Monotheism to satisfy the feeling or imaginative life, just a strong flavour of duty, prohibition and retribution. By transferring her own iniquity to me, and conducting my soul murder, Mother conferred sanctity upon herself and a closer communion with a god who may have been richer, cleverer and more powerful than she, but who was otherwise easily identifiable by a cultured member of the Jewish middle class. Much as I disliked God, I was not convinced he would have liked Mother.

In some parts of the world it has been usual for the sacrificial victim to be rent slowly to pieces, while in other parts the victim was quickly dispatched and just the heart reserved as the focus of ritual. In some societies, selected victims have been cast off to live apart from the community, for years on end, in mystic seclusion before being tossed on the pyre; yet others have been abandoned to the wilderness. In many of these diverse cases it has been commonplace for the victim to be related to the one who performed the sacrifice. Who better to represent the character of the parents than the child?

Mother's behaviour towards me contained all the elements of primitive sacrificial rituals. She attacked me physically and verbally; she assaulted me emotionally; she overwhelmed me spiritually. She murdered my soul – robbed me of my identity – by showing contempt for me and excluding me from family life and abandoning me to the wilderness.

These early experiences have left me in a constant state of doubt. I have never satisfied myself, for example, as to whether I wished more to be perfectly integrated into the family circle or utterly separated from it. I have never made up my mind which is the more painful: to reject or be rejected. Like many who have been abused as children, I maintain an unconscious need for punishment, combined with a sort of rebelliousness. I saw my parents behave without due regard to the morality and decency to which they paid lip-service: I saw them 'rebel'. I found myself inculcated with this strand of their contradictions. All I would resolve was not to repeat their infamy with a child of my own.

There was never any question of my being able to go to my parents to heal my pain or solve my problems: they were the cause of both. The true curse of this condition is that parental hostility denied me the opportunity to develop the inner resources I needed to defend myself from it. I was just not up to my parents' enmity. I was too small, too young to bear the unbearable. Mother displayed such self-mastery; she was implacable. Because I know now that her immoderate anger stemmed from feelings of impotence, and that her self was small, tight and unregenerative, makes no inroads in my own Lilliputian complex. Although I accept that I was not responsible for what I suffered at her hands, I am nevertheless left with a sense of guilt: my life is run by remote control.

I imagine that we are probably all born with an idealized image of 'mother'. I must have been. I seemed to expect exemplified generosity and warmth, a soft suppleness of the affectionate mother with all-enveloping arms. For when I watched Mother climbing out of the bath, naked, my reaction was much more than alarm at her stark nakedness. I felt terribly undermined. I saw a body scarred, flaccid, hirsute, exuding sweat, excrement and urine from mysterious and revolting outlets. I saw a face masked by the salt-white stains left by trumped-up grief. I was faced with a *reflection*, not an image. Because generosity and affection were absent from Mother's heart, they went unreflected in her body. What I saw was decay and corruption. I glimpsed death.

The years following Mother's death have been appalling. I never considered publishing my work on piacular sacrifice. In any case, my theories resembled psychological case histories rather than archaeological inquiries. I had an unsympathetic professor and he was not best pleased that, as he saw it, I had squandered his department's time and money on something I refused to pursue to a conclusion. I handed in my notice just before he gathered himself to hand it to me.

I made the pre-emptive strike about ten years ago. Since then I have been slowly destroying myself with cigarettes, alcohol and sleeping-tablets.

My narrow tree-lined street, first discovered and settled by Walter forty years past, has the air of one that shelters good folk from the Happy Families cards – butcher, baker, candlestickmaker. Today there are the Cypriot grocer, the Indian newsagent and the Irish launderette manageress. The residents pass the time of day and are always ready to help with blocked drains over bank holidays and with non-starting vehicles, no matter the hour. Since I first came here to live the road has been gentrified, but its character has not changed. In place of the poor, decent folk who were once my neighbours (where are they now?), well-heeled, decent folk have moved in. Many of the houses have windowboxes kept in perpetual bloom by young Sloanes with a gaily painted van. The street is lined with Porsches, Mercedes and BMWs, and the children who set off for school as I get up wear the uniforms of exclusive private schools. But just around the corner and across the way, things are very different.

Since Thatcher came to power, nowhere was this been more evident than in Hogg Walk. The Adult Education Institute, after whose founder the street was named, has been turned over to the manufacture of Christmas crackers. The houses present an air of defeat: dirty-windowed, torn-curtained, pock-marked stucco. Half have been repossessed by the banks and building societies, the others occupied by squatters. In the few in which the residents have been fortunate enough to find work – albeit work with unsocial hours – sixty-watt bulbs are lighted before dawn and left on all day, together with the TV set. Their small front yards do not support as much as a blade of grass but are littered with empty beer-cans, fag-ends, used condoms and excreta. The council does nothing to clean the equally dirty pavements and gutters in these bleak, dusty streets.

Daylight mocks Hogg Walk and the surrounding roads. Dark suits it better, we, the more fortunate, agree. Day and night down-and-outs doze on the public benches. Schizophrenics, discharged from mental hospitals on the outskirts of London into the community, shout in these streets; unmarried, unemployed Irish labourers drink themselves into forgetfulness or chat up the ancient, sick bag-women who haunt the same shop doors behind the market. It occurs to me that theirs could easily become my fate, for I have not yet made the journey from victim to survivor. Even the cats look mangy.

The passing of a decade imposes a penetrating significance which I cannot ignore. Since my sixtieth birthday and the first payment of my pension, I have wondered what, besides reaching this staging-post, I have achieved. The frail identity I salvaged from the tip on which my parents deposited it is hard to locate. Can I be a complete woman without a partner and without having fulfilled myself with a son or daughter? Undesirable and undesiring, what does it mean for me to call myself a woman? I stand naked before the looking-glass and observe an all-too-close resemblance to Mother reflected there. Like my body, my mind is crumbling. My powers of concentration are limited, my memory is failing. I can no longer refer to myself as an archaeologist when I have chosen to relinquish my job, having lost my taste for my subject. To identify myself as such would be as senseless as to carry on as if I were still a young girl. So, I am sexless and careerless! What is left to me but the past sixty years? And with their increase, all that will accrue is my further decline.

My collapse following Walter's death was severe, but nothing near as lastingly stultifying as my subsequent nullification. It is as if the cruelty of childhood – which, to some extent at least, I accepted as being something every child of unsympathetic parents goes through – reached its full horror only when it first became a component of loss, at Walter's death, and the absolutely impossible burden of today only when the accumulation of understanding has been brought to bear on Mother's and Father's actions. Now, when it is too late to exact retribution, I realize the full horror to which I was subject.

But now I am fully determined to be the author of my exile. For at last I know deeply what I am: a Jew. Not half a Jew, as I was taught, but altogether a Jew, according to the Beth Din, the Israeli government and all anti-Semites. I have 'the Right of Return' to a place from which I was exiled two thousand years ago . . . I am not dispossessed.

Returning has been my continuous mode of being. I have come to little understanding either in my work or my life, and am left with the unpalatable truth that only the past is certain and nothing can be undone. I returned to Mother. Where did that lead? Neither of us could accept its implications. I returned to the subject of human sacrifice in my work, only to discover that, in one way or another, it is as much part of the human condition as perpetuating the species. Over much of the world it is no longer required physically to sacrifice a victim for religious reasons. We can take him hostage, sexually abuse him, starve him, disinherit him – or organize mass murder for purely secular reasons.

It is since facing my chronic sense of nullity ('There is nothing to be afraid of, *Liebchen*') that I feel a sort of relief. I have discovered my identity: I am a microcosm of my race. My life has been precarious and threatened. I have been hounded and hurt. I have known rootlessness and exile. I might even go so far as to claim that I am victim of a family holocaust. In addition to the illness and poverty I see in and around Hogg Walk, the everlasting flame of hatred lighted two thousand years ago could catch up with me. The under-class is desecrating Jewish graves and setting fire to Jewish restaurants in London and the provinces.

I have served my sentence. I shall flee.

But a man set free from prison does not leave behind his guilt. I am connected to the central dilemma of the Jews for having accepted my fate without taking drastic measures to preserve myself against my aggressors. As a child, I made myself an accomplice of my parents by not exposing their abuse of me. I was their scapegoat just as the Jews have been the scapegoats of the Christians, and shuffled to their deaths as if their destruction were inevitable, a matter of fate, even the will of God. We Jews have been so inculcated with the judgement of those who wished us dead and forgotten that we have shared in the guilt imposed upon us by those who, with the authority of the Church, wished us abandoned by God.

Without my being entirely clear why, I feel pretty sure that the time has come for me to avail myself of my Right of Return. There are pressing negative reasons for my not continuing to live in England: the whole tenor has become antipathetic. If for no other reason than not having to listen to interviews in which cabinet minister and industrialists admonish the poor for making efforts to avoid slipping further into the gutter, I shall be pleased to be away. No society that caters so exclusively and with such self-righteousness to the thrusting, the selfish and the materially obsessed is pleasant to live in. At least in Israel everyone is united in having mere survival his most pressing need.

Post-Mortem

I think there is more barbarism in eating a man alive,
tearing him to pieces by torments and hells, than in
eating him dead.

                                                    Montaigne

If it should come to pass that men of other creeds and
nationalities live among us, we shall accord them
honourable protection and equality before the law.

                            Theodore Herzl, *The Jewish State*

I AM WRITING THIS IN ISRAEL. I HAVE SETTLED IN JERUSALEM, IN
an unmade cul-de-sac, in a rather disorganized neighbourhood
inhabited largely by oriental Jews disinclined to discard the merest
trifle that could be put to use in the battle for survival. Whatever
they cannot fit into their dwellings, they store in boxes and plastic
bags in their diminutive yards. Despite the unsightliness that
results, I prefer to live here than in the soulless *shikunim* beloved
by most immigrants from the West.

My house has two rooms. I had a bathroom built on and the
existing lean-to scullery improved. There is little land with the
house, just six foot round two sides, nothing where the bathroom
has been installed, and a larger area on the fourth side, overhung
by a truly magnificent fig tree. I would not want to dignify this
space by calling it a 'terrace', but it provides shade in which to sit
to work and eat. I have placed my old kitchen table and chairs
under the tree.

I brought with me few possessions: the kitchen table and chairs,
relics of Walter's and my daily life; Walter's old armchair and
cuttings from the *Liebchen* rose-bush; and all my books and papers.

I should have found house purchase impossibly difficult without
the help of Miss Harvitz from the Anglo-Saxon Immigrants'

Agency. Miss Harvitz has all the necessary flair for negotiating the maze of Israeli bureaucracy. Despite her mixed bewilderment regarding me in general and my wish to live in this area in particular, it was she who located the house – and the Arab carpenter and his son who built me cupboards, put up shelves, painted the wood floorboards and whitewashed the walls. Miss Harvitz did once inquire of me, in barely concealed tones of irritability, whether I had considered a kibbutz as my final resting-place. 'Some have very comfortable guest-houses.' I had, I told her. 'In my opinion, you might have done better to stay among your own!' she snapped. Miss Harvitz reminds me a little of Charlotte.

Both in their official and social capacities, people ask me what it was that made me avail myself of the Right of Return. I find that for every person who asks, I have a different answer. I mention, of course, my early wish to partake in the establishment of the state and, to some, I confide the problems that made it difficult for me, when I had no ties, to up-stakes. I also mention how, from the safe distance of England, I had felt a sort of affinity with Israel, a country under siege, surrounded by twenty-two hostile states and the ocean. (Like Israel's, had not my own transgression been my quest for independence?) With the handful of people I know quite well – and this includes Professor Yehuda – I do admit that the ambivalence I have experienced throughout my life with all that concerns mother country is at the root of my decision. Before I left England it had occurred to me that it might be possible for one guilt to be displaced by another, in the manner that a chronic anxiety is forced aside by a more acute one, and one obsession by another. I wondered whether the guilt visited upon me as an abused child might not be transferred to real and actual culpability. I was, after all, becoming a citizen of a country whose political, military and human responses to its subject population sickened me. By taking up my Right of Return, was I not tacitly condoning what I deplored? And would this ambivalence not take precedence over other feelings?

But I never confided, even to those I knew well, the precipitating experience that controlled my final decision.

I had been recommended some German papers on child sacrifice and chose to go through them in the Reading Room at the British Library. I had been reading since quite early in the morning and by about 2 p.m. I had reached the final short account – a coda – with which the collection was rounded off. In this piece Professor Steinberger recounts the history of Hans, born prematurely and physically deformed. His mother, an under-age farmer's daughter, had successfully concealed her pregnancy from her immediate family, insisting that her size was due to her uncontrollable appetite for food. She was never to divulge the child's paternity.

RS (as she was referred to throughout) gave birth, alone, in a disused shed well away from the farmhouse. It was only her superstitious nature that stopped her from suffocating the baby at birth, and it was probably her dull intelligence, as much as her shame, that was responsible for Hans's being undernourished as a baby. When he showed signs of being ready to crawl, RS chained him to a stake in the locked shed and passed oddments of food to him through a hole in the wall. The little boy was left soiled, cold and lonely for most of the day and all of the night. This imprisonment continued until he was about five. It was only when an official from the Agricultural Ministry was sent to the farm to investigate an unrelated matter and forced open the shed for inspection that the horror of Hans was exposed.

Hans was immediately allocated a social worker and taken into care. His mother was imprisoned. His grandparents, genuinely innocent of what had been going on, were settled in sheltered accommodation. The farm was sold.

The institution into which Hans was put was somewhat overcrowded and, unlike others which might have been more suitable, was not divided into small houses where each child received individual attention. When Hans was eight, his case was reviewed. He could count to ten with the assistance of his fingers and he could do a few menial tasks – pack shelves, empty bins. He had learnt to talk monosyllabically, and to eat with a knife and fork. He had made no friend; he could not (or would not) look anyone in the eye, and he shunned all physical contact. He was small for his age, badly co-ordinated and very spotty. The institution was probably correct in believing that they could do no more for Hans and that his best interests would be served by his being adopted into a family setting, if one could be found, carefully supervised by a local social worker.

However, it was discovered that Hans's maternal uncle and his wife were living in Bavaria and Hans could not be adopted outside the family without the consent of this uncle and of the grandparents.

It was obviously for financial reasons that Uncle Conrad and Aunt Maria refused to consent to Hans being adopted. The grandparents blackmailed them: if they took in Hans, they would inherit; if they did not take in Hans, they would not.

Uncle Conrad and Aunt Maria lived in a two-bedroom house, one of which was unoccupied and promised to Hans. A place was secured for him at the local village school, three miles distant, at which the headmaster, with a backward child of his own, would make Hans welcome.

The little boy must have realized that all was not well from the day he arrived at his uncle's house. Instead of the room which he had been promised, and which featured large in the mind of a child who had known only a shed and a dormitory, he was ushered into a store-room in the basement, next to the boiler. His bed was a straw mattress on the floor. He was given no toys or other possessions of his own. Aunt Maria refused to have anything more to do with him than set his breakfast before him, before he left for school, and his tea on his return. She infrequently washed his clothes, and the children at school complained to the headmaster not only that Hans sniffed continuously and murmured incoherently under his breath, but that he smelt. Uncle Conrad was less wholly dismissive of the child than his wife but he was acutely stern: he beat Hans if the child did not do at once as he ordered. Hans learnt to obey his uncle's wishes, partly to avoid being struck and partly because he appreciated the moments he spent alone with his taciturn guardian in the fields, at market, and listening to the radio.

The walk to and from school was long for a child with one leg four inches longer than the other. Hans was always tired and often slept through his lessons. His teachers made allowances for him but did nothing to investigate his family situation. Now that Hans was legally adopted by the Schmidts, the social worker struck his name off her list of children at risk.

It did not occur to Hans to report that he was being bullied by the children at school. He had come to accept that his deformity, his spotty skin, his ragged and dirty clothes lent themselves to contempt and violence from others. He had never experienced affection and did not imagine it was owed to him.

One late afternoon, returning from school in the dirty half-light of November, Hans heard a mewing in the ditch. He dropped down the slope to the edge of the stream where he found a kitten. The little half-drowned animal was as thin and frail as himself and had no doubt been discarded for the same reason that he had been. It had a broken leg and patches of furless skin. Hans picked up the kitten and concealed it under his shirt, close to his heart, and took it back to his basement room.

At once, he set to whittle a stick of kindling for a splint and tear a strip from his shirt for a bandage. Tenderly, he set the kitten's leg. Then he made a bed of rags for the animal to sleep on, in the warmest corner of the room and, in the opposite corner, he laid newspaper on which he taught the cat to soil.

Hans showed a skill and cunning in tending his kitten's injury and feeding it that he had not achieved in any other area of his life. Indeed, overcoming the problem of how to get food for his pet became his first cherished and fulfilled desire. His love for the animal gave him a sensation that was new to him and joyous. It was remarked at school that he had started to smile and would initiate a conversation, even though he had very few words at his disposal with which to further it.

It was probably as much as five weeks before Uncle Conrad, returning unexpectedly to the breakfast table, discovered Hans pouring milk from his mug into a medicine bottle. Hans could have lied: he could have said that he was going to take it to school. But he was not a liar. He told Uncle Conrad about his cat and he told him how much he loved his animal. He went to great pains to explain to the man – despite his few words but with the help of gestures – that the cat was not doing any damage, or making a mess, or costing anything because all its food came from his own plate.

Uncle Conrad seemed to swell in size and turn beetroot red. He called the child an idiot, and an ugly, verminous, unwanted idiot at that. He was nothing but a liability his uncle could well do without. Seizing the child by the scruff of his neck, he dragged him down into the basement. He had not given permission . . . Hans was a drain on his family . . . stupid, ugly and would come to nothing. Bastard! he yelled, and while he yelled he struck the child across the face. 'You're no good at anything, not in the fields, not at school, not in the house. . . .' And then he let go of him and threw open the door to Hans's room. Hans froze to the spot at the open door and watched his uncle leap on the little cat sleeping peacefully on its rag bed. He watched as his uncle picked up the animal and with one massive hand on its front paws and the other on its back paws tore the cat in two.

Disorientated, I rose from my seat. I picked up the journal and groped my way, holding on to the backs of other readers' seats, and then to the general catalogue fixture and, somehow, returned the journal to the appropriate place and person. I wandered out of the Reading Room and, dazed, forgot to offer my bag for inspection. I was called back by the attendant. Crossing Great Russell Street I was aware of a motorist only narrowly missing me, calling out after me: 'You mad or something?'

There was no question of my returning home. That I knew. At the same time I also knew that there was nothing to detain me in town. I felt myself imprisoned in a carapace of pity and terror.

My breath was short; I felt I was suffocating, unable to breach the iron bars of my thoracic prison. With the image of Hans's first ten years of life incised on my consciousness, all I wanted to do was to flee: flee from the feelings this image aroused in me. I started walking.

It was 3 a.m. when a policeman stopped me in a street in Kennington and asked me if I was 'all right'. Where did I live? Should he call a taxi to take me home? I gave him my address and accepted his offer of a taxi. I was quite unable to account to myself for the hours between four in the afternoon, when I left the British Library, and three the following morning, when the policeman roused me from my sleep-walk.

The story of little Hans remains with me but nowadays it is the resolution of his experiences of cruelty and rejection that detains me. The day after Uncle Conrad tore his cat in two, Hans shot and killed his uncle with the weapon the man used to shoot game.

Hans was committed to a reformatory. Such language as he had acquired gradually deserted him. He regressed. He used his fingers to feed himself and he never looked anyone in the eye again.

I have discovered that I am closer to other abused human beings than I am to the powerful. And I experience a fierce sense of vicarious satisfaction when I hear of abused children who take their revenge on their abusers rather than on themselves. For a split second the abiding feeling of infant desperation lifts. And so I set out for Israel on the side of the underdog, but not knowing, a priori, which underdog would detain me.

Before settling here, I visited six times, five for my work and the sixth to explore the country as a tourist. Perhaps, unconsciously, I had had it in mind to settle, eventually. But since the early fifties, when the experience of Walter left me indifferent to just about everything else, I seemed to have been detached from Israel. When visiting Israeli historians and archaeologists came to see me in London, we always discussed what was going on in the Middle East, whether they were apologists for their government or critical of it. Thinking back, I remember that these conversations always left me confused, with jostled feelings of anger, sorrow and disappointment. It was rather as if we had been discussing family matters.

I remember early on feeling decidedly cheated that Israel had substituted nationalism for Zionism, and capitalism for socialism. Nor could I sympathize with its racism: Jews from Morocco, Algeria and other Arab countries had – and have – about the same status here as blacks from the Caribbean in Britain. And if this was not bad enough, I knew that Israel exported racism by supplying arms to dictators in the Third World, and white South Africans with the razor-wire with which they corral black South Africans into slum compounds. Whereas I used to dismiss this sort of practice as being no more than one could expect from the British, that they flouted sanctions against South Africa and operated race discrimination in jobs and housing at home, I clung to a lingering idealism that made me expect more from a Jewish state.

If I hoped that by coming here I could escape my past, I was mistaken. I have re-entered it – through a different door. What I endured in my parents' house is what the Palestinian endures in Israel. The historically abused Jew has, like most abused children, become the abuser.

Where human sacrifice is practised, flesh is strength and enemy eating increases the consumers' powers. It is the consumption of the heart, however, that constitutes the blood covenant, designed to ratify allegiance with the gods. My own soul murder combined both these strands. Mother identified something in me that was powerful which she lacked. It was almost certainly the spark of identity that Father's very early love for me had engendered. To gain this for herself, Mother first had to implicate Father in my inquisitorial sacrifice, and then get him to justify the whole charade on the grounds that I was a threat. For Mother pretended that I was as dangerous as cholera, degenerate mentally, and physically displeasing. And, as I have shown, went to pains to have her diagnosis corroborated. Sometimes she accepted a metaphysical explanation for my condition, sometimes a psychological one. For her, I was the sort of impure child that Gabineau, Nietzsche, Darwin, Wagner and Hitler would have had sacrificed. Mother satisfied herself that her calculated destruction of me was valid for being the only way that someone pure and blameless has to survive in the face of someone evil.

Vilifying your enemy is a strategic first step in its destruction – a fact that has not been lost on the Israelis, who pour scorn both on the intelligence and the sensibilities of the Arabs. 'They are liars and thieves from birth!' Punishing your enemy for reacting to your abuse is often the second step in its destruction – a fact that has not been lost on the Arabs, who in defending themselves have found themselves labelled 'terrorists'.

The Palestinian has been colonized. By annexing his property and denying him self-determination, Israel has reduced the Arab population within its bounds to an abject condition, one that in turn arouses Israeli contempt and provides an alibi for further denials of human rights. This circular syndrome is a well-tried one. Other aggressors in our time have used it to justify their misrule and tyranny, with similar results.

Now the Jews have their own 'Jews'. Morning and night, night and morning, a steady stream of Arab men flow up and down the main highways. These men are going to work on Israeli building sites and in Israeli factories. The houses they put up they will not live in; the goods from the factories in which they sweat will be too expensive for them to buy. Like all subject people, they toil as menials for their masters and are feared as much as they are loathed. One of the problems faced by an abused child is that his abuser may also be his provider, and without him the child could dissolve altogether. The Palestinians must be taught to confront this problem and not work for the Israelis.

I am reminded of parental self-righteousness. The Israelis, adopting an expression of fraudulent hurt and incomprehension, ask why it is that the Arabs do not conform to their perceptions of what is good for them. 'If only they would behave as we behave. . . .' 'If only they would see how fortunate they are to live in the only democracy in the Middle East. . . .' But Arabs are not Jews and do not behave like Israelis, nor do they benefit from Israeli democracy. Nor do they want social and political solutions imposed upon them. They want a state of their own in which they can labour for themselves. They want to re-establish their identity. And for making these rights self-evident, they are accused of terrorism.

Self-righteousness means that the oppressor can never admit to being in the wrong. What he fails to notice, however, is that the primitive ritual of sacrifice he expects to lead to his renewal leads to his spiritual demise.

The Israelis cannot admit to the Palestinians' having any rights without fearing their own destruction as an outcome. This was Mother's problem: were she to allow me my identity, she felt she would lose her own. But more than that, if she admitted the wrongs she did me, she feared that I would not forgive her, that I would avenge myself upon her, and so I had to be destroyed before I brought about her annihilation.

Israel is simply internalizing the repressive and destructive treatment meted out to Jews world-wide, the remnants of whom it was founded to succour. Like the most typical abused child, Israel manifests anger and hate and an awesome lack of concern for others, particularly for the 'other' in its midst. The fact that these negative feelings may be the outcome of two thousand years of rejection and worse does not make Israel's behaviour anything other than delinquent. And the more the world remarks the fact, the more Israel kicks the dog.

The State of Israel and the Arab world are no more likely to be reconciled than are the abused child and its parent. Like the parent the state dares not admit that it was the prime mover in what ensued. Incontrovertibly – whether there were extenuating circumstances or not – Israel was founded at the expense of the Palestinians: it annexed more of their territories in 1967 and integrated them, and is even now settling religious fanatics on Palestinian soil. Partition is unlikely. In all the confusion that is the political situation here, I am profoundly aware that, facing my abused race, I see nothing but an abuser.

I am seated at my table under the fig tree. It is early evening. The relentless heat of the day hangs about in vegetation burnt dry as a mummy. The grey stone under my feet is stained purple from the blood of overripe fruit.

I got back from the north three days ago. I went to visit Professor Yehuda. Shortly after he retired, he was widowed and decided to return to live on the kibbutz where he had been born. His invitation to me was for the Sabbath which, in Israel, constitutes the weekend. However, in the event, I stayed four days. Professor Yehuda's letter of invitation had been more discursive than letters I had received from him in the past. I had the impression that the retired academic had time on his hands. 'Would you be bored by an old man?' he inquired, rather coyly I thought. 'It is no longer my work that detains me these days,' he added.

The road to the kibbutz climbs steeply, winding around hills terraced for almond, orange and peach trees. At the crest of one hill I could see that an archaeological site had been excavated. In the dazzling light of summer, which robs the landscape of much of its colour, I could just make out the contours of a few Arab dwellings huddled together and, below the group, the gaping mouths of caves. Way down in the valley was a lush green place, the outlet of a spring of water. It must have been this source that had provided the focus around which Naveh Shalev had been founded. I called out to the bus-driver and asked him how much further it was to the kibbutz. On being told that it was a little over a mile, I asked him to stop at the next passing place. I would walk.

It is almost unbearable to be alone in such beauty. I picked my way along a stony path and every few yards stopped to look out over the land. A deep silence broken only the chirp of cicadas prevailed. As I stood to listen, I breathed in the scent of wild fennel. On the horizon, the cultivated land stopped abruptly at the desert plain, behind which rose a mountain with a table-top. All that confronted me had unforgettable majesty. A cupola of blue hung over the world of Israel. A few streaks of white, torn off clouds from elsewhere, reminded me of the formidable odds that had made bringing this land to fruition such an act of faith.

This is a land of extreme contrasts. In places it is lamentably unkempt; litter blows about on the hot winds and fastens itself to prickly weeds abundant in the waste lands. In the towns garbage collects stinking in the gutters. In other places all is fastidiousness,

158

burgeoning with fruit and vegetables, the produce seeming to shine with pleasurable gratitude for the loving care lavished on every plant, bush and tree. These extremes of difference in the maintenance of the material world are reflected in the people themselves and their allegiances. In the towns there is stress and a frantic competitiveness: the people have substituted material gain for self-fulfilment. On the *kibbutzim* something of the founding socialist, humanitarian ideals survive.

Naveh Shalev was settled in the early part of the twentieth century. The inhabitants of the little Arab hamlet nearby had not at first been hostile to the foreigners, who assumed ownership of the caves. The spring in the valley was generous; there was enough water for everyone's needs. But as the settlement grew, and shacks with an air of permanence about them proliferated, so did hostility. Some of the founding fathers died of disease, some of exhaustion. There was malaria and there was dysentery. Bodies cut adrift from the stock of Talmudic scholars, tinkers and tailors withered, pulling fruitless trees out of the rocks, clearing swamps, digging irrigation channels, mixing concrete, ploughing, planting. . . . And then, when the locusts came in storms and laid waste the little that had come to fruition, some took their lives. Only the brawniest of the men and the most obstinate of the women carried on. It was among their number that Professor Yehuda had found his parents.

He told me how he revelled in the rhythm of the week and of the year: the inevitability of the ploughing, sowing and reaping; the inevitability of the rain, cold and heat. He laid stress on the fact that at Naveh Shalev the members and the land they work still co-operate to meet a common end. 'It is tacitly understood that the collective will is a more worthy cause than the individual will.' This, in a world dominated by self-interest, was an inspiration to him. He told me that he felt he was much more precisely fulfilling his parents' purpose now – grading fruit and helping with the accounts – than he had been working at the university. He said that he could understand why it was that many born on Naveh Shalev could not aspire to its ideals. 'We understand, the individual is conflicted. He feels the need to realize himself personally. It's not enough for him to play in an orchestra, he wants to be a soloist.'

Professor Yehuda asked me whether I had noticed the caves ·in the hillside to the east. He told me that when his parents arrived in the valley, they had installed themselves in those lairs and lived in them for a full year while they gathered materials to erect wooden shacks. And he walked me across the dusty ground of the compound and showed me six nicely conserved dwellings standing in a eucalyptus grove.

'Imagine, a couple were overjoyed to share such accommodation! We've travelled a long way since. . . .' And he reflected on those early settlers, the seriousness with which they took life, the zeal their mission afforded them. 'How horrified they'd be to see those who administer their legacy today.' Professor Yehuda's parents and their friends had been poor Zionists, from the *shtetles* of the Pale, but there had been others among them who had fled from assimilated families in Germany, with wealth and power, precisely to escape the values that now prevail in Israel.

We spoke of man's confrontation with nature and how this cannot be achieved alone. We talked about the work in which we had been involved in our professional lives and how it could not be resolved alone. Listening to Professor Yehuda, a man who saw further than most, I felt my own threshold widening and deepening.

'Our role in history is an active one. We are no longer a movement but a state. We stand to be judged on the world stage by the most exacting standards.' His voice rang out like that of an Old Testament prophet.

Professor Yehuda occupied a two-room flat on the ground floor of one of the recently built blocks of flats grouped round a quadrangle, reserved for elderly members. I was reminded of the cloisters in Italian monasteries. In the heat of summer the lawn was lush emerald green thanks to concealed sprinklers. Some of the flower-beds were looked after by the children of Naveh Shalev – they reserved them for biblical plants. Others were radiant with the flames of bougainvillaea. I thought back to the past, to the cracked, dry land that the professor's ancestors had nurtured so passionately. What was it that had turned some of their children into men like him and others into brutish materialists and vulgar avengers?

'In the morning I rise at dawn to watch the sun melt the mists on the hills. At dusk I walk to the edge of our land and feel the hills close in maternally. This is truly paradise.'

Lights from the flats shone out on to the quadrangle but did not invade all the corners. We sat watching shadowy figures quietly come and go. In the half-light we found it possible to confide.

I was surprised by the intemperateness Professor Yehuda displayed. It was something he had not previously revealed in my presence. It crossed my mind that the very old may regard it as a treat to show this excess, when other treats are no longer available to them. But then I realized that in the past our conversations had been about matters not directly concerned with him. In his retirement he had become completely overwhelmed by what he saw as the descent into hell. He expressed disgust for Israeli values based on competitiveness, and profit and loss, and made an assault on what currently fills the gap once occupied by fraternity.

'Israel', he told me, 'lost its struggle for self-preservation in the communal experience when it modelled itself on Western suburban life. It substituted for it the mere struggle to survive. It's as if the state had been obliged to create an external enemy to provide the rampant selfish individualism with something of the flavour of fellowship.'

I saw that his anger weakened him physically. I understood why, after a bout of fire and fury, he put unaccompanied Bach on his record-player and sat, his hands folded across his stomach, with his eyes closed. He needed to gather the forces of peace about him. But when the music came to an end and he rose to fill my wineglass, the first thing he said was that Herzl would be struck dumb if he were to walk down Dizengoff Street today.

'He'd only have to sit in a café to learn within five minutes that no one trusts anyone, that violence is never more than a stone's throw away, and that guilt is abiding.'

Without being an observant Jew himself, Professor Yehuda spoke as affectionately of the old religious *kibbutzim* as he did of the old secular ones. But of the new settlements, the extending limbs of colonialism, he spoke bitterly. As we drove more deeply together into the past and reflected on its influence on the present, Professor Yehuda indicated that he saw a striking relationship between Israel's history of feuds, of colonization, of arrogant superiority and contempt for others, and my family life. 'As an archaeologist, as curators of the past,' he mused, 'it is imperative not only to lay bare the evidence but to relate it to its context, to compare it with other contexts, and to record it.'

In one of his bouts of disgusted despair, Professor Yehuda

complained: 'We have broken faith with people in our care.' This was the nub. 'On the West Bank and in Gaza, we've closed their schools and universities. Are we going to burn their books? It's as if we want to keep them uninformed so that we may accuse them of ignorance. . . . I was walking in the hills. I stopped to talk to an old Arab farmer. He told me that he wanted to plant three fig trees for his three great-grandchildren. But to do this he needed a permit and he'd never get it. Well, he might or he might not. That's hardly the point. These people are living without rights and in fear and degradation – as we did for two thousand years. . . . Now, it seems, it's their turn to live in a world without joy, without continuity, without meaning.

'I've seen our soldiers shoot stone-throwing Arab children. Like the English shoot rabbits. They regard them as vermin.' And he described what he had seen: children left to lie in pools of blood and with shattered bones; mothers and fathers tumbling towards them, risking being shot at themselves if they try to retrieve the bodies of their children for burial. 'There is a connection, I believe, between our having lost our collective will and administering collective punishment. We burn down the houses of people suspected of having a relative involved in terrorism! Since when has collective punishment been acceptable in a civilized country? This is the behaviour of the South Africans, the South American dictators, Hitler. . . . It's the lives of our own men that are no longer worth living. A negative cause is no cause at all. They have become oblivious of what they are doing. They do not see that they are being robbed of their humanity.'

While Professor Yehuda spoke, rather as if to himself, I recalled the awe-inspiring wailing of distraught Arab women that I had heard from my own house close to the old city in Jerusalem and being conscious of the pall of hatred that hangs like a low mist over us all after a particularly loathsome incident.

Professor Yehuda took down from his shelves a huge volume of Jewish history and two books of fiction by Elie Wiesel. We fell to talking about the words of violence and scorn that seem to be the very building blocks of Jewish experience. We counted forty words for physical abuse – for the various tortures suffered by our people – and thirty for contempt and derision. It seemed to us that the Jews had worn thin words for suffering. It was then that Professor Yehuda told me that recently, in X – and he named a small town to the south – a man had been sentenced to life imprisonment for the death of a child in his care. The man had been the director of a children's orphanage. In pursuit of sexual gratification he terrorized little boys as well as girls. Finally, one died as a result of some particularly perverse act of his and the man was exposed. The whole country had been scandalized; there had been a deluge of letters to the press, demonstrations, discussions on television. 'He was a survivor of the camps.'

In the silence that followed this revelation, it occurred to me to consider whether we Jews were going to persist in settling for no more than two choices: to put down roots in the diaspora, kow-towing to the ruling class to ensure our safety, or take up the Right of Return and find ourselves implicated in the destruction of others.

Before I left England, Helen asked me how I thought it possible to emigrate and settle comfortably somewhere so different from what I was used to at my time of life. Despite her work overseas, she regularly returned to base. Her roots lay deep in the secluded village in the Chilterns, in the bluebell carpets of the beech woods and the close-cropped hills where sheep graze. She slipped back into her mother's house and routine as soon as she set foot in the porch because, in some way, she had never left that threshold. By the morning after her plane touched down she was walking the dogs, making jam for the Women's Institute market and drinking sherry with the vicar. I tried to explain to her the alien feeling I had always had in England. She looked askance, clearly feeling uncomfortable. I did not press on to explain that, in addition, all my memories of childhood – unlike hers – were painful. I did not have the luxury of being able to nourish myself on the pleasures of birthdays, Christmases and family holidays.

I promised to write as soon as I had found a place to live. It was a difficult letter to compose – once I had finished describing my house, the road in which it stands and a little about the sort of life I am living. I felt defensive. Finally, I found myself relating an incident that summed up something I had found consoling about Israel. I hoped she would understand. I could not be sure.

One winter it snowed in Jerusalem and a small child who had never seen snow before gasped in sheer wonder at the trans-formation it wrought on the view from his bedroom window.

He was growing frantic with impatience to get out and play in the soft white strewn over the land. 'Let me go and roll in the stuff,' he implored. His mother, convinced he would catch his death if he did such a thing, took the washing-up bowl on to the roof and filled it with snow for her son to play with in the bathroom.

Despite my feeling that this mother was turning snow into an educational toy, I nevertheless found the story touching. I wondered whether Helen would understand why.

I came here to redeem my existence. Now I am here, I recognize in Israel something that belongs to me – something from which I have been separated. In England, since Walter died, I felt not only the loss of someone I knew and loved deeply but nostalgia for something I never knew. I sense that these feelings will slip away from me here. Despite the political chaos, the threat of hostilities and the brutalities of colonization, I shall stay on. These are matters simple in their translucence. I shall oppose them. When I was a child my preoccupation with justice and truth was taken as just another example of my insolent contrariness and I have no doubt that my pursuit of them here will meet with a similar response. But the weight of authority does not frighten me now. I disdain all authority that does not merit respect. The lesson of Father helped with that. And the completing something with which Israel provides me is a sort of love, and that stirs me with desire and energizes me. I have found a third choice. . . .

For sixty years in England my life lay along an emotional San Andreas Fault that enfeebled me, the way all senseless suffering enfeebles its victims. Here I feel vigorous: the prospect of suffering in a worthy cause is positively enticing. I shall be involved! In the old days, the time-space between the present and my memory of Walter had been the void. After Mother's death, despite short bursts of energy and subsequent short bursts of activity, I always sank back and experienced emptiness as the overwhelming reality of my existence: nullity. It was this that soured my relationships with colleagues and friends, making them seem futile. It was this that made the world seem purposeless. Nothing that was to be done in the immediate present detained me convincingly enough, and for a long enough period, for any achievement to result.

I had learnt before Walter's death what death was like. I had already experienced the feeling of having been cut in half and of finding everything in life meaningless because I had no one to share anything with. And then I learnt not to confide in others for fear of showing a dependence from which they might shrink. These were feelings that dissolved in our love affair, but they coagulated again when Walter died. My mind and feelings iced over.

What I am experiencing now is the thaw. Professor Yehuda listened at length and without interruption to descriptions of my childhood ordeal.

He asked me outright questions about Mother, Father and Charlotte. Whereas once I would have felt distress, having to resurrect material I chose to repress, I noticed that now I was feeling supreme indifference. I thought back to the day I walked into the garden when Mother was dying. . . .

What was it, Professor Yehuda wanted to know, that I remembered most vividly about Father? How would I sum him up?

'A man with all the subtlety of spur and whip.' But I smiled, for into my mind there floated the image of Father aiming a blow at my leg, missing, hitting the table-leg and flinching.

And of Mother?

'A witch. If she had a conscience, it never reproached her.' And my thoughts went back to the sight of her emerging from the bath. But instead of a feeling of nausea, one of pity overwhelmed me.

And Charlotte?

'All imaginative possibilities were bleached from existence by her mere presence.' And I recalled her as a creature of habit, dominated by her watch and a short list of social conventions. 'Anyone with the role of fly-on-the-wall would have been able to predict that she would benefit from my misery.'

I was conscious that none of it mattered; I was no longer in their power. That feeling has persisted. As I sit here, feeling alive to the tips of my fingers and toes, Mother and Father are just small piles of bone, their flesh which so abused my own eaten by worms. No doubt Charlotte keeps photographs of their graves and pays to have flowers laid on them by menials on the anniversaries of their deaths.

I have promised to keep in touch with Professor Yehuda and to keep notes for him on the work I am to do. I have accepted two assignments. One is to report to the European Community Investigation on the conditions in which child detainees (Palestinian) are held in Gaza. The other – he fully appreciates – is too secret to commit to paper. I *know* that I am putting myself at risk but I do not *feel* that I am being put at risk: that is the difference. The sense that I am acting out of my own volition, in a cause that I know to be just, is exhilarating. I am going to be part of a movement that will unleash the underdog, something it has taken me far too long to effect on my own behalf. It is this that I style 'The Third Choice'. It is this that gives 'mother country' a whole new significance.

Postscript

Extract from the *Jerusalem Post*, 26 November 1990:

. . . One of the Arabs involved in the shooting of Israeli passengers on the number 17 bus from Jerusalem to Ein Karem in September has admitted that it was he who killed Miss Antonia Sinclair, a recent British immigrant. The Arab, who has not been named, informed an interrogator that the woman was quite obviously working for the secret police or she would not have engaged in conversation with him. He regarded his crime as an act of war.

We have learnt from another source that Miss Sinclair was innocently visiting old friends who live in Ein Karem. We are informed by the couple that Miss Sinclair was not, so far as they were aware, involved in any political work. 'She was a professional archaeologist absorbed by a subject – human sacrifice – that always drew her back into the past. She had come to Israel to retire.'